D1826933

Golden Journey

A TRUE LOVE STORY

ERNA M. HOLYER

REVIEW AND HERALD® PUBLISHING ASSOCIATION
HAGERSTOWN, MD 21740

Copyright © 1997 by
Review and Herald® Publishing Association
International copyright secured

The author assumes full responsibility for the accuracy of
all facts and quotations as cited in this book.

This book was
Edited by Jeannette R. Johnson
Designed by DeLaine Heinlein-Mayden
Cover art by Joel Spector
Typeset: 12/13 Optima

PRINTED IN U.S.A.

01 00 99 98 97   5 4 3 2 1

R&H Cataloging Service
Holyer, Erna Marie, 1925-
    Golden journey.

    Series: Vienna Brooks Saga.

    I. Title.   II. Series: Vienna Brooks Saga.

        813.54

ISBN 0-8280-0964-3

Dedication

To Nan,
a wonderful friend and exemplary mother . . .
One of those precious friends one is fortunate to
meet, and a mother who has admirably reared eight
children, just as Eliza Ann Brooks did.

Contents

Introduction

Vienna Brooks, the heroine of this book, made the grueling wagon trek from Michigan to California in 1852. During her journey she fell in love with a golden young man from whom she became separated.

She considers herself engaged to him and prepares for the time when she will be John's wife and business partner. Will John wait for her? Will he come and claim her as his bride, as he said he would? She fights back doubts, while everybody discourages her.

Mother wants her to become a teacher and sends 16-year-old Vienna to academy. Well-heeled suitors come to court her, but she clings to her promise and the vision of one day marrying John.

At the academy she meets Priscilla, her childhood friend, who urges her to marry a rich man. Vienna is pulled in two directions. Her family has fallen on hard times, and a well-to-do son-in-law would ease their lot. She hopes that her brother, Elisha, will fulfill their mother's dream and become the teacher in the family.

Just when she thinks she has finally located John, she gets bad news. The hopelessness of her situation hurls her into despair. How she solves her problems is detailed in this book, the second of "The Vienna Brooks Saga."

Much of the material for *Golden Journey* was derived from published and unpublished reminiscences of Vienna's brother, Elisha Brooks. Without him the memory of Vienna would have been lost.

I wish to thank Mr. Brooks S. Whitney, grandnephew of Vienna Brooks, for the use of these materials.

Erna M. Holyer
San Jose, California

There is no photo of Vienna Brooks among the family records.

Chapter One
Roar in the Night

The last red ember in the cabin's large stone fireplace faded into gray. Vienna Brooks listened to the snores, even breathing, and occasional coughs of the sleeping people around her. She could barely see the crumpled shapes of the five boys and five adults lying under their worn blankets. Vienna herself lay wedged in between her two youngest brothers.

The 6-year-old to her right moved. "I'm hungry," he whimpered.

"Hush, don't wake anybody, Orion." Turning, Vienna bumped into 4-year-old Elmont on her left side. The boy awoke.

"Mama, I'm hungry," he cried.

"We'll soon eat, child," Mother replied in a sleepy voice.

Vienna pulled up her blanket. Her innards rumbled, and the thin layer of straw on the hard floor did little to cushion her body. She groped for her bundle underneath the pillow and felt for her diary. She had been wanting to bring it up to date, but there wasn't any privacy. Nearly two months had passed since her family took refuge at the Berry Creek sawmill after running from a snowstorm that threatened to bury them in the Sierra Nevada. Thinking about John, her golden hero, she sighed. Dreamily, she put her head onto the pillow.

Noises ended her reverie. Oxen, mules, and the pony began moving around in the area behind the lean-to. The mill hands stirred.

"Gotta get up! Gotta get that grizzly!" The three lads dove into their clothes and dashed outside.

Vienna arose and got a fire going. In the bright light of the flames, she saw that Father was getting up.

"Is there any breakfast?" he asked.

"Sorry, Pa, we're out of everything."

"Then I had better climb up the mountain and find that snowed-in pack train Slim spotted yesterday." Father bundled up.

"You're not well enough to wade through deep snow, Pa. Let me go instead."

Father laughed. "A girl? You'd be sorry."

Eleven-year-old Elisha darted out of the straw. "Let me go, Pa! I'll find that train. I'll get provisions."

"No, son. Bargaining with traders is a man's job. There's money at stake." Father left by himself.

Gunshots echoed from canyon walls. In a short time, the mill hands returned. "We missed that rabbit," they complained.

Vienna's stomach growled. As she mended Elisha's ripped jacket, she yearned for a bite to eat.

The cabin door opened again and the twins entered, clasping green bundles. "Here are good yarbs, Mother," Elijah said. He and his brother dumped the greenery into an iron kettle. Mother cooked the pungent herbs over the open fire, then ladled out the steaming soup.

"With the Lord's blessing, this soup will sustain us until more substantial food is found." She stood tall in her patched and faded dress. Her voice was brisk, her enunciation perfect as three lads, five boys, and a girl gathered around the crude table.

Mother seemed to be chilled, and drew her shawl close about her shoulders. Brown hair, center-parted and gathered at the neck, framed her drawn features. Her oval face showed hollows below the cheekbones. Vienna gave her mother a searching look. Mother needed nourishment. She was spoon-feeding little Elmont, sharing her own ration, as usual.

Vienna added to Mother's blessing. "God always provided for us on the overland trail. We must thank Him for the good food He's sending our way."

Mother smiled.

The mill hands' unhappy glances showed that they despised the soup. Wedged in between the members of the Brooks family, they appeared ill at ease. Slim was their spokesman. Sonny and Sam spoke when spoken to. The sturdy fellows boasted fuzzy blond beards and hats they kept on, even at the table. Vienna remembered how the brothers had looked aghast when her family appeared at the cabin door. Nevertheless, they had shared their winter's supply of beans and hardtack until provisions ran out. Now the lads dashed outside to try their luck again.

Father returned, bent forward and staggering under the plump sack on his back. "The pack train was a couple miles up the road," he reported. "The trader sold me 50 pounds of flour." Father let the sack slide onto the table. His steel-gray eyes blazed.

"What happened?" Mother asked.

"Fifty pounds of flour for $50!" Father was angry. "Robbers! Thieves! They took advantage of our need."

Mother laid a firm hand on Father's arm. "We must thank the Lord for the flour and all the good meals we'll enjoy, dearest. Let us bless this flour and forget about the money."

After a meal of flapjacks, Elisha announced bad news. "The oxen are gone. Help me look for Nig and Brock!"

Vienna hurried outside. The pony greeted her with joyful nickers. The four mules met her with flopping ears.

But where were the oxen? She checked behind the lean-to, peered through wagon wheels, and considered sloshing downhill.

The cabin overlooked the sawmill, stacks of cut lumber, and the stone dam that held back the millpond. Runoffs gushed past the lumber stacks, and the road was filled with slush. The water's roar was deafening. Vienna turned back.

"I don't see the oxen anywhere, Elisha." She shouted to make herself heard.

"I'll check the other side of the rise, sis." Elisha trudged uphill.

"Your brother is still looking," Vienna told Elijah in the cabin. "Why don't you go with him?"

But Elijah didn't stir from the hearth. He looked at her with scared brown eyes. "Slim said there's a grizzly around. Do you suppose the grizzly spooked the oxen?"

"I hope not. Listen!"

Shots cracked, and the mill hands' jubilant cries resounded outside. She jerked the door open and saw the lads dragging a large, shaggy animal downhill by a rope. Elisha scrambled downhill behind them, tears tumbling over his hollow cheeks.

"Nig is dead, sis!" He rushed past Vienna to the lean-to and emerged with a bundle of hay he had tied into a piece of canvas.

"Where are you taking that?" Vienna asked.

"Old Brock won't come home. I must feed him, or else he'll starve."

The next day Elisha carried another bundle of hay to the ox. "Brock won't leave Nig," he reported upon his return. "He's defending Nig against a pack of wolves. Brock hates wolves, always has." The boy swiped at his nose with his hand. "We must bury Nig."

Vienna blinked back tears. "Slim, Sonny, and Sam are busy with their bear," she reminded her brother. "And Father needs rest."

Mother broke in. "Why don't you ask the lads, son?"

"Bury an ox?" the mill hands grumbled. "That boy's crazy!" Nevertheless, they exchanged butcher knives for picks and shovels.

Bundled up against wind and rain, the family walked beside the young lumbermen. Vienna was thankful Father had offered to stay behind with Orion and little Elmont. She felt a pressing need to attend the ox's funeral. Mud squishing underfoot, she plodded up the mountain trail. A skyward glance showed clouds racing above swaying tree-tops. A storm was blowing in from the Pacific Ocean.

On the crest of the hill she braced herself against wind and rain. Collar turned up and bonnet tied close to her chin, she glimpsed Nig's lifeless body. Brock was charging into a flock of wildly scattering crows and magpies, who rose up in a screeching flutter of black and white, then settled on nearby branches. A dead wolf lay nearby, gored by Brock's sharp horns.

The old ox greeted the family with angry snorts, then chased the mill hands into the woods. Elisha slowly approached the ox, reassuring him with gentle words.

"You can come out now!" Elisha called to the mill hands.

But Slim yelled from the safety of a tree trunk. "We can't bury your ox. Let's go home afore Brock gores us."

Elisha held up the rope he had brought along. "Come under, Brock!" he coaxed.

Out of sheer habit, Brock trotted toward the boy and swung his long horns under the imaginary yoke. Elisha fashioned a noose around the ox's neck and tied him to a nearby branch. Mother's smooth talk kept Brock as docile as a lamb.

"You can come out," Mother informed the mill hands.

Slim, Sonny, and Sam dug in haste, casting worried glances at the tied-up ox. After covering Nig, the lads slapped the rain from their hats and turned to leave.

"That's it," Slim declared. "See you at the cabin."

The boys wept. "We can't leave Old Nig like this,

Mother," Elisha said. "We must do what's right."

Mother stepped to the edge of the rock-covered mound. "You would do us honor if you stayed," she pleasantly informed the mill hands.

"Y-yes, ma'am," they said. They took off their hats—and stayed.

"Let us derive comfort from the Scriptures, children." Mother's voice rang clear as a bell. "Our good and faithful Nig has passed on to his reward. We say goodbye to our dear Nig with as true a sorrow as we ask for our own last hour. God bless you, dear Nig. We thank you for your faithful service."

Elijah stepped beside Mother. "Our good friend Nig went 'Gee' and 'Haw' to our journey's end. God bless you, Nig."

Elisha stepped beside his twin. "When we were 9 years old, Pa gave us each a yearling calf. No boys ever felt so rich and important as we did, knowing we owned beings that had life. We rode astride their backs. We harnessed them with ropes. We yoked them to our sleds and hauled our winter's wood."

Vienna grasped the cold hand of Justus, the family's middle child. Her voice failed her. She tried again. "Our dear Nig pulled us through the wilderness with his fading strength. He saved our lives and never deserted us. God bless you, Nig. We will remember you as long as we have breath in us."

The mill hands wiped their knuckles over red eyes and hurried off before Elisha released Old Brock. The ox sniffed and snorted around Nig's burial mound and refused to leave. The mourners started homeward without him.

"It's all right," Mother soothed. "Brock will follow us when he is good and ready." She put comforting arms around the twins as they strode toward the rise. "We have each other, children, and we have Father. Jehovah blessed us richly. Let us look forward to the future."

Vienna lowered her head against the gale-force wind. Through streaks of rain, she saw the churning water in the millpond. Fed by runoffs and rain, the creek had been swelling for weeks. Scum and uprooted trees tore over the rock dam, and the spillway roared under a cloud of white mist.

Back at the cabin the mill hands cooked bear steaks over a smoking fire. Fat sizzled on the crackling logs as Slim held out a chunk of meat at the end of a fork.

"Have some," he offered.

Vienna's stomach lurched, and she fled the cabin. Mother coaxed her inside with the promise of a meal of flapjacks. In the smoke-filled cabin, the girl reached for her moccasins, feeling cold and miserable.

The gale screamed around the cabin, rocking its foundation. By nightfall the storm hurled tons of water against walls and roof. Gusts shrieked down the chimney, fanning glitters of sparks and showers of ashes. A tree came crashing down, and branches broke.

The storm reached great fury after midnight. Drumming rain assaulted the cabin. Whimpering, Elmont crawled under Mother's blanket. Orion clung to Vienna.

"You are safe," she comforted.

A loud noise made Vienna jump. The roar was like an earthquake, like thunder, like a hundred cannon shots fired all at once. Vienna thought it was like the trumpet call announcing the end of the world.

"God save us!" Slim cried.

They rushed outside at dawn. Rocks ground and crushed against one another in a wild rush of water. Logs and pine trees swirled downstream. A pile of boulders, scoured clean by the raging water, showed where the sawmill had stood. Matted grasses indicated where the stacks of lumber had been stored.

Father struggled to salvage bits and pieces. Pain distorted his pale face, and his words expressed despair. "A fortune is floating down the river," he lamented. "Two years' work washed away! That lumber was supposed to pay for our milk business down in Bidwell Bar. Now we're flat broke."

"We shoulda grubbed for gold," Slim said bitterly. "Hey, George, we're going back inside. No use trying to save that scrap. Come and have a steak with us." The mill hands hastened to the cabin.

Mother joined Father quietly. She sent Vienna back to the cabin. "You'd best get out of the rain," she said gently.

Shivering in her wet clothes, Vienna headed for the dry cabin.

Slim stood by the hearth, holding up a bottle. "Let us toast the New Year!" he cried. "So long as a pioneer lives in Butte County, California, he'll remember this sodden winter. Let us toast our future as gold miners!" Slim's laugh sounded like a sob. "Here we come, skilled lumbermen, joining the fools who stand in the stream rocking the miner's cradle."

New Year's Day! Vienna had forgotten about the twins' birthday. This was 1853. Elisha and Elijah were 12 years old.

Chapter Two
Gold Rush Boomtown

One brisk April morning, Slim, Sonny, and Sam packed their mules and left. Father snapped out of the despair the lumber loss had hurled him into. He made repairs on the wagon, readying the vehicle for the 12-mile journey down to the Bidwell Bar mining camp.

There wasn't much to load up. Mother added tools and tents to their clothing, bedding, cooking utensils, and the books they had managed to save.

Ready to leave Berry Creek, they said goodbye to Brock. The ox hadn't come near the cabin since the night the grizzly scared him off. They found him chewing his cud in the clearing where Nig lay buried.

"Come under, Brock," Elisha coaxed. The ox spurned the imaginary yoke Elisha held up and charged Father, who attempted to lead him to the wagon.

"It's no use," Father said. "He's going to gore people."

Vienna and her brothers bade Brock a tearful farewell. Elisha hitched his pony and Father's mule to the wagon. Mother handed up the younger boys and boosted herself onto the wagon. Vienna rode up front with Elisha, who acted once more as their teamster.

The wagon, canvas top patched and mended, jolted over the rutted, washed-out road that connected the high country with Bidwell Bar. They traveled in a canyon beside a wild, roaring stream. Then the trail wound past cool ferns and moss-covered rocks where flower cushions burst forth from rocky crevices and morning sunlight glinted on freshly leafed-out bushes.

Vienna drank it all in. "We're making a new start in the mining camp, Elisha. We must pull together because Pa is sick," she said. "We must work hard so that our family is good and settled when—" She stopped herself.

"When what?" Elisha struggled with the brakes. They were descending fast.

"When I get married."

"Married—you? Aren't you too young?"

"I need an education first, Elisha. I want to be a smart bride."

Elisha looked puzzled. "Where's your groom?"

"I don't know, but I'll find him."

The canyon widened, giving way to an expanse of turbulent water. Suddenly gripped by fear, Vienna called into the wagon. "Pa, you didn't tell us about this big lake."

Father stuck his head out. "Well, I'll be!" he exclaimed. "The middle fork of the Feather River! It's flooded beyond belief!"

Vienna's legs had turned to jelly. The roaring river had inundated the countryside. "How do we get across?" she asked in a small voice.

"Over the foot bridge, kitten. Do you see that floating bridge? A raft is fastened by ropes on both shores."

"No, Pa," Vienna quavered. "All I see is water."

Mother stepped behind the girl and put both hands on her shoulders. "I am glad there is no bridge, daughter. I should refuse to entrust my children to this turgid stream."

So a year after leaving their Michigan home, the family was camping again. While waiting for the flood to subside, they dug wild onions from the ground and harvested local plants. Vienna watched the river from the gravelly knoll on which they had pitched their tents.

On a balmy May day three weeks later, a boatman took Father and Elisha across. When Father returned by himself, Mother's face went white.

"Where is Elisha?" she asked.

"I tell you, that boy has spunk," Father chuckled. "Our son will find a job and earn some money."

"How is he going to get back?" Mother asked.

"I gave him a quarter for the ferryman."

"But Pa," Vienna interrupted, "what can Elisha do? He's never had a job before."

Father laughed. "That boy can handle a team, he can shovel dirt, he can sell merchandise. It's all arranged, kitten. Before long we'll get our new home, and the boys will go to school."

"School?" Vienna's hopes rose sky-high. "Is there a school in town, Pa?"

"Not yet, but they'll get one, and a teacher too." Father rubbed his beard with obvious satisfaction.

"How do you know?" Vienna persisted.

"I know because I'll build the schoolhouse, and your mother will teach. Now what's to eat?" Father turned to the biscuits and onion stew Mother had saved.

One warm July morning Vienna helped the family break camp. The last spokes of the covered wagon fueled the breakfast fire. Ducks broke from the backwater, and quail sounded rallying cries. Vienna hummed as she rolled up her blanket. Suddenly she let out a screech. "Who took my diary?"

When Justus ran away, she chased the mischief maker around the ring of hot stones and wrested the diary from him. A dried rosebud fell out. Vienna quickly retrieved it.

"Who gave you *that?*" Justus teased.

"None of your business," Vienna scolded, placing the rosebud carefully between the pages.

"Well?" asked Elisha, who was taking the day off from working for a gold miner.

"It's from John." Vienna felt herself blush. "Help me look for a tall, blond man with beautiful white teeth and a great smile, Elisha. He rides a chestnut mare."

Elisha dismantled the twins' tent. "Does Mother know you're sweet on John?"

"She does—sort of," Vienna sighed. "She said I'm too young to even think of marriage. Oh, Elisha, if only she had listened to John!" She brightened. "I can wait. I need an education first, academy or college."

"Does that cost money?" Elisha asked.

"I suppose." Vienna glanced at Mother, who was putting pots and pans into a piece of canvas cloth and tying it shut.

Mother straightened up. "What are the two of you whispering about?"

"Oh, nothing." Vienna wrapped the diary and put it into her bundle.

Mother bounced little Elmont in a rare display of exuberance. "We shall have a real home again," she told the little one.

Father looked up, smiling. He was strapping tools and other hardware onto the mule. Elisha took Elmont from Mother and hoisted the boy onto his pony. Orion sat on the mule. Carrying bundles on their backs, the members of the Brooks family marched to the ferry. Fish jumped in the river, and miners panned for gold along the banks.

The boatman frowned at their baggage and grumbled about transporting useless little boys. It required several trips to get them all across. Elisha held the rope while his spunky Indian pony swam across beside the boat. Mother ferried over with the screaming Elmont. Vienna entered the swaying boat with Orion. Her knees shook as memories of crossing the flooded Missouri came back. Justus and Elijah ferried across together, laughing all the way. Father came last with the mule in tow.

Reunited at a place called Frenchman's Garden Fence, Mother knelt down in prayer. "Let us thank the Lord for guiding us safely across yet another flood," she said.

The miners doffed their hats to Mother. Vienna discreetly scanned the bronzed men, answering Elisha's questioning look with tiny head shakes. Bidwell Bar was booming. Horseback riders dashed about. Wagons loaded with barrels and boxes rumbled through the streets. A blacksmith pounded his anvil. Crews of men were leveling building sites. It was a man's world; there was not a woman in sight, Vienna realized.

Father stopped at the money exchange. "Time to trade in Elisha's wages," he said, and entered with Mother.

The banker himself escorted Vienna's parents out, showing Mother utmost respect. "It will be an honor to have you as Butte County's very first public schoolteacher," he said.

Mother smiled, and Father looked proud. Vienna's parents next entered a merchant's establishment. Vienna peeked inside, heart pounding. The store was stocked with boots, trousers, red-and-blue flannel shirts, slouch hats, suspenders, and overalls. The proprietor hunched over the counter, scribbling figures on a pad of paper. Vienna stood transfixed. She imagined John behind that counter, and herself beside her golden hero. When the proprietor looked up, she turned away, waiting in the plaza's dazzling sunlight until her parents came out with their purchases.

Two miles southwest of the gold rush boomtown, Father unhitched the mule. His arm swept over a most agreeable area. "This is our place!" he announced. "We have pasture, wood, and water. It's the place I've had my eyes on."

"It isn't ours until it's paid for," Elisha spouted.

Father laughed. "We'll pay back the loan in no time, son."

Mother drew the boy aside. "You must show respect for your father," she admonished. "Have you not learned from the Scriptures that the man is the head of his household? His wife and children must obey him. You must honor your father, Elisha."

Elisha kicked at pebbles. "You did all right without him, Mother. You never borrowed any money."

Mother looked stern. "Have you forgotten your lessons from the Scriptures? God made Adam first, then Eve."

"I'm sorry, Mother. I'll be more respectful. I'll honor Pa," he promised.

A cabin replaced the Brookses' tents during the summer of 1853. Father showed the twins construction tricks he had learned back East. Working with handmade mallets, templates, wood chisels, and broadhead axes, he practiced his skills with pride. Before long, the twins chiseled out mortise and tenon joints and fashioned scarf joints to splice timbers together.

New emigrants and their stock poured over Beckwourth's Pass. They helped Father and the boys raise the roof on the family's new home. Father traded his mule for a milk cow and a sturdy pony for Elijah.

During the dry summer months the twins helped the gold miners when Father didn't need them. The miners diverted the river's flow to reach the gold-laden bedrock. Not far from the miners' tunneling, a schoolhouse went up and townsfolk took up subscriptions so they could pay Mother $50 for each of the three months she agreed to teach.

In the rainy season Mother taught the primary grade and Vienna took care of things at home. At the end of her three-month term, Mother didn't renew her contract because a new baby was on the way.

The day the baby arrived, Mother said, "Let us record this day, April 18, 1854, for this is a new beginning."

A week later Elisha laid a copy of the newspaper and a bunch of wildflowers in front of Mother. "The *Butte Record* printed an announcement about little Jay," he explained.

Mother sat comfortably propped on a pillow with the baby at her breast. "Read it to me, Elisha."

Elisha cleared his throat and rustled the paper. "Why don't you read it, Mother? The print is kind of small."

Mother smelled the flowers. She seemed to be in no hurry to read. "What are you learning in school?" she asked.

"Nothing, Mother."

"Why not?"

Elisha's lips curled. "The teacher is useless and cruel, Mother. Children hate him. He's dirty and slovenly, and people say he drinks whiskey in a cave across the river. Mornings, he summons his pupils by beating an old tin pan. He beats his pupils with a stick, Mother."

Mother put the baby aside and grasped Elisha's hand. "You must attend school and learn, son. I fear you have forgotten how to read."

Vienna felt sorry for her brother. He hadn't been able to take much time out for school, what with working for the miner and doing odd jobs around town.

A short time later, she was flabbergasted to read in the newspaper about a school strike. And Elisha was involved. "That boy!" she muttered.

One sweltering August day a fire originated on the corner of Water and Miner streets. Fanned by the wind, the inferno consumed the town's wood-and-canvas houses within an hour, leaving untouched only the courthouse, the ferry, a boardinghouse, and the newspaper building.

After the flames died down, Vienna and her brothers helped the townsfolk salvage what few things had been spared by the fire. Through the curtain of smoke and flying ashes, they recognized a familiar figure, coughing behind a cloth pressed against his nose and mouth. They watched as the town's highly unpopular teacher prowled among the ruins and carried off a roasted dog.

The next day boys and grownups entered the teacher's

cave. After hearing the men's report and the boys' testimony on Courthouse Hill, the sheriff drove the worthless teacher out of town. With the teacher gone and the schoolhouse burned to the ground, Vienna's brothers didn't care if they ever heard the word "school" again.

Soon after the big fire, the canyon echoed with the thunder of hooves. Horses whinnied, cattle bellowed, sheep bleated, and drivers yelled. Father stood in the doorway, propped up on the homemade crutches he had been using lately.

"How many animals are you moving?" he yelled at the trail boss.

The man reined in his horse and pulled down the red bandanna that shielded his mouth and nose from the dust. "Set out with 500 horses, 1,200 cattle, and 700 sheep. Lost a few though."

"Have you got any milk cows?" Father shouted.

"The best! These cows will improve the California stock. Pasture and good water will bring on the milk in no time."

Father saddled up a pony and rode into town. When he returned, Mother asked questions. "Is it wise to take out another loan, dearest? Can we pay it back?"

"No need to worry, dear," Father chuckled. "When those udders fill up, we'll be in clover. Miners and townsfolk pay for milk with gold."

"What if the gold gives out and miners move elsewhere?" Mother's forehead showed a steep worry line.

Father waved off her concern. "The gold hasn't been tapped yet. New deposits are turning up constantly. The town is being rebuilt in stone. We'll have new hotels and mercantile establishments, stage lines, boardinghouses, and theaters."

Mother frowned.

"There's talk of incorporating as a city," Father continued. "Everything will be bigger and better. What's more, a great suspension bridge, the first in the West, is coming to

Bidwell Bar. The pieces will be shipped from San Francisco, then freighted by wagon to Frenchman's Garden Fence." Father shifted his weight on his crutches. "The bridge will open the high country to wagon traffic, and all the world will pass through this town. That means progress and prosperity!"

"I hope you are right, dearest." But Mother's feeble smile did not relax the steep line on her forehead.

Chapter Three
In the Gold Mines

Get up, boys; 'tis three o'clock!"

Father's voice jarred Vienna from her sleep. Elisha crawled out of his straw mattress and fetched the milk pail.

"Elijah, get up!" Father called.

When Elijah moaned, Mother checked on him. "The boy has a fever," she said. "He better stay home today."

"Cows must be milked and people must eat," Father admonished.

Vienna peeled herself out of her blanket. "I can go, Pa!"

"No, kitten. A girl in the mines is no good."

"They won't know I'm a girl, Pa." Vienna groped for her brother's jacket and pants.

Mother looked thoughtful. "With her hair tied up and hidden under a hat she may pass for a boy," she said.

"I guess we have no choice." Father did not sound happy.

Vienna milked alongside Elisha. She poured the frothy liquid into cans, then dropped the cans into canvas bags behind the pony's saddle. Side by side, sister and brother rode into the town.

They tied up the ponies at the plaza and wrested the

cans from the bags. Gray morning light trickled into the ravine as they separated, each carrying cans of milk to various miners' shacks, tents, and cabins along the river's long gravel bank.

The miners, young and tanned, were a motley crowd from every part of the world, judging by their strange talk. Elijah served some rough customers, Vienna realized. A wild bunch banged away with six-shooters, while others slept on their gold. None of them appreciated a trespasser on his claim. She stepped carefully over mine tailings, tools, and debris.

"Hey, boy, who are you?" A miner pulled a dark brown cake from his pocket, bit a piece off the smelly thing, and chewed the wad.

Vienna disguised her voice. "I—uh—my brother is sick. He'll be back tomorrow." Heart pounding, she poured milk into the container the miner held out without spilling a drop. Bulging muscles protruded from the miner's red flannel shirt. With his pants tucked into huge boots, he looked like a rough-and-tumble sort.

"Didn't mean no harm, boy." The miner pinched Vienna, making her wince. He laughed and spit out black tobacco juice. "You're so skinny a fly would slide off ya, boy."

Vienna pushed the miner aside. She collected her pay and moved on. Miners ate cooked beans with coffee, or washed down their dried and salty meats with milk.

At the end of the camp she saw a brawny giant who slept outside on a buffalo hide. Since she had some milk left, she woke him.

Startled, he reached for his gun. "What do you want?"

"It's m-me—the milk boy," Vienna stuttered.

"You don't sound like him."

"I, uh, my brother is sick." Vienna pulled her hat down over her face.

The miner put his gun down and paid for a pitcherful of milk.

The girl hastened back to the plaza. Elisha wasn't back yet; his pony was still waiting. Vienna had milk left over—she must have missed some of Elijah's customers. She let the empty can slide into the pony's canvas sack and dragged the other can from door-to-door.

Bidwell Bar looked more prosperous than ever before, she reflected. Mr. Gluckauf, the merchant, had erected a fireproof building. At its grand opening, people had made good-natured jokes.

"It will last," they said.

The National Hotel was rebuilt. Dr. Wilson and many others had erected bigger and better structures after the fire of the previous year. A brickyard, completed last spring, turned out handsome bricks. The bakery, livery stable, and blacksmith shop stood in new glory around the plaza. Houses of stone, express companies, stages, hotels, and theaters. And soon a mighty suspension bridge would open the high country to wagon traffic. There was no end in sight to the town's prosperity. Father's prediction had come true, she noted with satisfaction.

The Bidwell Bridge company had dumped huge iron pieces from the Troy Iron Works of New York near the ferry landing. How Mr. Evans, the engineer, fitted the pieces together puzzled Vienna. But Mr. Evans was smart, and the great man himself had engaged her brothers' services. Mr. Evans was paying her brothers a quarter dollar for each pound of lead foil they brought to him. Tea arrived in bales wrapped in great sheets of lead. Proprietors gladly saved the sheets for the boys, seeing that the bridge would bring new business to town.

Vienna sighed with pleasure. The twins were saving their money for her education. Whistling a tune, she sold the last drop of milk.

The sun was riding high. Time to herd the cows. She helped Elisha with the herding during the long, hot day. After evening milking and her second milk delivery in the mining camp, Vienna felt too tired to eat. Her muscles ached when she went to bed at 9:00.

The next morning she was greatly relieved when Elijah responded to Father's call, "Get up, boys; 'tis three o'clock!"

It was wash day. Vienna rubbed her aching muscles. At last the wash fluttered on the line strung between two pines. Shirts, pantaloons, diapers, and skirts hid Mother from view. Baby Jay rocked in his crude playpen in the shade while Vienna cooed to him.

Hoofbeats startled her. Who'd be coming to the Brooks Ranch at this time of day? she wondered. The twins weren't due until late evening.

"Is anything wrong, Elisha?" Mother called as Elisha slid from his pony.

"I brought you a bunch of flowers, Mother."

"God bless you, son." Mother sniffed at golden poppies and purple lupines, smiling happily.

Elisha rummaged in his pocket. "I started to write a poem, Mother. It isn't very good though."

"Let me see!" Mother took the crumpled paper Elisha handed her.

Elisha gave her no time to comment on misspellings or bad penmanship. He began to recite:

"On Feather River's brink I stand,
A youth with raven locks.
Reflected in the limpid strands
I see today white rocks."

"Dear son, you give me great joy." Mother's crisp language contained a wealth of warmth.

Elisha grasped her hand and pressed it against his cheek. Vienna watched the scene between Mother and son, hot tears welling up in her eyes. The months on the overland trail had forged a bond between them stronger than the steel cables that would soon hold up the new suspension bridge.

"What can I do to help you, Mother?" Elisha asked.

Mother hugged him. "You are doing more than your

share, Elisha. No boy your age should be called upon to work so hard. You ought to be able to sit in school and learn."

Hammer blows behind the house stopped. Father's crutches clunked out of the cabin, and the spell was broken. Elisha sprang on the pony's bare back.

"Wait!" Father called. "Are you telling your mother that you have to work too hard? Are you complaining?"

"N-no, Pa."

"Let me tell you something," Father said. "My little brothers, myself, and my cousins worked in the woolen mills and cotton-cloth industries of New England. We supported the family at an age when you were still sledding for fun in Michigan. We rose before daybreak and went to bed after dark. We didn't enjoy the luxury of fresh air. We worked in the stale air inside and under tough bosses. We worked!"

"Y-yes, sir, Pa," Elisha said and rode off in a hurry.

Vienna felt sorry for her brother. Father was strict with the boys, but the twins were doing their level best. She felt guilty. The twins were saving every extra dollar they earned for her education at an academy, and she had no idea how she could pay them back. She wished she could discuss her problems with a girl her age. Priscilla Wilson came to mind. Vienna sighed. She had lost contact with her childhood girlfriend.

Chapter Four
Surprise Visitor

Vienna looked up from the scrubbing board as a horse and buggy approached. She dried her hands on the apron hugging her slim waist and brushed wispy brown hairs from her damp forehead. A gentleman driver came into view. Forgetting the scrubbing board and basket of wash that stood ready for hanging, she flew up the road. Her heart sang. Maybe John had found her at last!

The driver pulled back on the reins. "Whoa!"

Disappointment washed through Vienna. This dapper young man wasn't John, her golden hero. Collecting herself, she spoke politely. "Are you lost, sir? Do you need directions?"

"Lost?" he laughed. "Certainly not! This is exactly the place I'm looking for."

Vienna shaded her eyes against the high August sun. "Who are you, and what do you want?"

He laughed out loud. "Don't you remember me, Vienna Brooks? I am Jeffrey."

"Jeffrey who?"

"Your former teamster, that's who!" He threw his hat on the seat, jumped from the buggy, then guided the horse into the shade of a pine tree.

She barely recognized the beardless, fair-skinned lad who had driven her family from St. Joseph County, Michigan, to the Missouri River. His jolly eyes still danced, but the home-styled haircut had yielded to a barber's grooming. The sandy hair was pasted to his temples where his hat left red streaks. His upper lip sprouted a fuzzy little mustache, fine blond hairs that didn't show up much. He hadn't grown much taller, she noticed. Only his mustache indicated that time had passed.

She groped for words. "How long has it been?"

"Three years," he said.

"How did you get to California?" Vienna asked. "You didn't cross the Missouri like the rest of us."

"That's a long story, Vienna. Fortunately, I'm here and I found you." He set the brake and fastened the reins. "Let me look at you!"

Vienna felt dizzy as he whirled her about. "Let me go!" she protested. As he set her down she picked up a whiff of tobacco smoke.

"You're the girl I remember, Vienna Brooks! Silky brown hair, flawless skin, a voice like a bell. How old are you now?"

"Sixteen."

He beamed. "I'm glad I came up from San Francisco."

Vienna's hand darted to her mouth. "San Francisco? The place they call the wicked city by the Bay? Is that where you live?"

He grinned. "It's a good and prosperous place."

She had to ask. "Do you smoke tobacco?"

"Not me! I leave that dirty habit to others."

"Strange . . ."

"I guess I shouldn't have stopped off at that saloon. I needed directions."

"How did you find me?" Vienna asked.

"By chance. A gold miner in San Francisco bragged about having seen the prettiest girl in Bidwell Bar, a mining town in Butte County. The milk boy told him your name."

Vienna snickered. She had instructed the twins, Elisha and Elijah, to advertise her name in the mining camp, hoping that John would learn about her whereabouts. Obviously, the boys had been doing a super job.

She studied Jeffrey's clothes. Aside from people like the banker, few men around Bidwell Bar wore vested suits, white shirts, and elegant cravats.

"You're not a miner, are you?" She felt foolish for asking.

"Certainly not!" Looking smug, Jeffrey unbuttoned his jacket. Vienna couldn't miss the boastful golden watch chain draped across his vest.

The door of the log cabin creaked open, and Mother stepped outside. She was bouncing a blond, curly-haired toddler. The wide-set eyes in her oval face narrowed at seeing Jeffrey. "Whom are you visiting with, daughter?"

Jeffrey stared at the tall, slim woman at the door. He didn't give Vienna a chance to explain. His manner changed as he respectfully addressed the girl's mother. "Mrs. Brooks, ma'am, your former teamster has come to visit old friends."

"Jeffrey?"

"Yes, ma'am! Figured I must apologize for the, uh, speedy manner in which I departed."

Mother's face tightened. "What else brings you here, Jeffrey?"

"Business, ma'am. I hear Bidwell Bar is a good place for doing business. Being the county seat and getting a suspension bridge that will soon allow wagon traffic to the high country, the town is bound to attract new business."

"What kind of business are you in?" Mother appeared to be in no hurry to invite the visitor into the cabin.

"I am catering to the needs of gold miners, ma'am."

"Selling equipment and such?" Mother gave him a penetrating look.

Jeffrey brightened. "And such. I bring greetings from the

Wilsons, your neighbors back in Michigan."

Vienna screeched. "You saw my friend Priscilla?"

Jeffrey nodded. "After turning back from the Missouri, I dropped in at your neighbors'."

"What did the Wilsons say?" Mother shifted the toddler to the other arm.

"That they missed you at the Sabbath service, ma'am."

Vienna interrupted. "Did Priscilla miss me?"

"She said she did. In fact, she pestered her pa to pull up stakes and head for California."

"What did Mr. Wilson say?" Vienna held her breath.

"He wasn't keen on it."

"And Phil, what did he say?"

"Priscilla's brother? Not much. He's a quiet one."

"Wouldn't it be something if we saw the Wilsons again, Mother?" Vienna turned hot and cold, thinking of her childhood friend.

"How did you like Priscilla?" she asked Jeffrey.

Jeffrey shrugged. "A spoiled kid used to getting her way. Would you believe she threw a temper tantrum right in front of me? She stamped her feet and made the red braids fly!"

Vienna giggled. "That's just like Priss. Why was she angry?"

"Because her pa didn't want to take her to California."

"And Mrs. Wilson," Mother broke in. "Did you meet her too?"

"I certainly did, ma'am. Now there's a city-type woman, nice-looking and very generous. I hope Mr. Wilson appreciates the fine woman he's married to."

Mother cut off Jeffrey's prattle. "And you, Jeffrey, how did you get to California? I didn't think you would—" Mother didn't finish the sentence.

Vienna knew Mother never forgot the bitter hardships the family had endured on their grueling journey—hardships they suffered because of Jeffrey's desertion.

Father appeared in the doorway, his crutches making clunking sounds. "Is it time to eat yet?" he called. Then noticing the visitor, he fixed a surprised gaze on Jeffrey. "Who are you?"

"A Michigander like you, sir, a former lumberman. Back in 1852 I drove your family all the way to the Missouri River." Jeffrey contemplated the stocky blond man on crutches with a look of astonishment.

"That so?" Father draped husky shoulders over his crutches. "What brings you here?"

"A desire for health, wealth, and happiness, sir."

"Health and wealth?" Father scoffed. "I'll have you know there are sick people in California too."

"I'm sorry, sir. I had no idea you're an invalid."

"Never mind that, young man. What adventures brought you to the Golden State?"

"Returning from the Missouri, I drove a wagon heading east, then worked my way to Massachusetts," Jeffrey said. "I found employment on a sailing ship and came by way of Cape Horn, sir. You can't imagine the terrible voyage on that small ship. Rough seas and scurvy-sickened passengers and crew. Many died for lack of fresh food."

"That so?" Father's voice rose to a higher pitch. "Let's go inside and eat," he offered.

"Thank you, sir!" Jeffrey respectfully entered the cabin behind the family.

Two blond boys looked up from playing with wooden blocks. The younger boy ran screaming out the door.

"What's the matter with him?" Jeffrey asked.

Vienna answered. "Poor Elmont is 7 years old and still afraid of strange men. Somebody scared him on the wagon train."

"I am not a stranger," the visitor asserted. "I am Jeffrey."

"Jeffrey?" Orion, the 9-year-old, wrapped himself around the lad's pant legs. "Are you coming to live with us again?"

Jeffrey laughed. "He remembers me."

Vienna pointed to a seat at the table, then turned to Mother. "Do you want me to go after Elmont?"

"Leave him be, daughter. We'll feed him later." Mother's voice was gentle.

Vienna doffed her apron and slid onto the bench across from Jeffrey. "How did you get to stay in San Francisco?" she asked. "Weren't you supposed to sail back on the ship?"

"Sail back? No way!" Jeffrey shook himself. "I jumped ship while unloading whiskey barrels. No way was I going back to that stormy South American cape. Ships are known to founder around the Horn."

"What did you do ashore?" Vienna prompted.

"I teamed up with two fellows I had met on the ship," Jeffrey explained. "The three of us started a business at the waterfront."

"Catering to miners?"

"Miners and sailors." Jeffrey stirred the steaming soup Mother had ladled into his bowl. "Why stand in the river washing gold? There's more gold in business. My plan is to buy out my partners. A banker in San Francisco lends money to enterprising young men. With a loan from him I can have my own business, take all the profit, and prosper."

Father plucked at the beard he no longer bothered to trim. "How will you spend your money, if you ever do get rich?"

Jeffrey jumped at the question. "I'm gonna build myself a mansion on one of those San Francisco hills and marry the prettiest girl around," he gushed. "I'll be a gentleman, and she'll be my lady. We'll be rich, and people will respect us." Pausing, he looked around the modest cabin. "If her folks need money I'll be happy to help out," he added.

Vienna blushed. Everybody was looking at her. "What about church?" she stuttered.

Jeffrey shrugged. "She can take the carriage to church anytime she wants to."

Mother passed out freshly baked biscuits. "What about

the Sabbath, Jeffrey? Can you keep the Sabbath with all your high-flying plans?"

Jeffrey tasted the soup. Giving Mother a polite smile, he said, "This soup is wonderful, Mrs. Brooks, and these biscuits look great. You always have been a good cook." He turned to Father, ignoring Mother's question.

"And you, sir? How are you getting along?"

"Can't complain, Jeffrey." Father adjusted his suspenders. "I'm in the milk business, having bought some milk cows."

Jeffrey turned to Vienna. "Didn't you tell me your father was in the lumber business?"

Father took over. "I was, but fate took a different turn."

"What happened?"

Father's gray eyes dimmed. "It's one of the things a man doesn't want to talk about."

"I am sorry I asked, sir. Forgive me. I had no idea you ran into bad times." Jeffrey looked puzzled.

"What's past is past, Jeffrey. We made a new start. The family works together, and we're doing all right." Father smiled at the toddler on Mother's lap. "Only this little one doesn't pull his weight. All he does is eat and cry," he joked. "Jay was born here in California."

Jeffrey clucked. "You're a lucky man, Mr. Brooks. You have a fine wife and a lovely daughter. Apart from your health, you seem to have a good life."

Father smoothed his beard, uttering a sigh. "There is one problem."

Jeffrey leaned forward. "Oh?"

"Our daughter wants to attend a girls' academy."

"Academy!" Jeffrey clucked.

"We'd miss her, Jeffrey. She's a help to her mother and a comfort to me."

"I can see that, sir! Anybody would like to have a girl like Vienna around." Jeffrey turned to Mother. "How do you feel about this, Mrs. Brooks, ma'am?"

Mother quit spoon-feeding the toddler. "I would like for

Vienna to consider a teaching career, Jeffrey. Children need moral guidance. Without knowledge of the God-given laws, this land of ours will be a lawless country."

Vienna changed the subject before the matter got out of hand. "Do you still have the gun you bought at Council Bluffs?" she asked Jeffrey.

"Sure do." Jeffrey reached under his black broadcloth coat. He pulled a gun from its holster, twirled it in the air, then stuck it back with a flourish.

Father stared. "Are you a marksman?"

"I get by."

"Let's go find out." Father left the table, ignoring his crutches. His walk was jerky, and he groped for objects to hold him up. Orion, who was crazy about men's company, ran after him.

Why had Father left his crutches? Vienna wondered. Did he want to impress Jeffrey? Did he feel flattered by the young man's attention? Or was there some other reason?

"Why do you think Jeffrey bothered to find us?" Vienna asked her mother.

Mother put baby Jay into his pen. "He is curious about you, daughter. Jeffrey is scouting for the best girl a fellow can buy." Mother cleared the table, frowning.

Vienna returned to her laundry, mulling things over. Jeffrey had brought back memories of the westward trek, memories of her childhood home, memories of John. Jeffrey had sailed all the way around the tip of South America. He had jumped ship. He had made the lengthy journey from San Francisco to the Brooks Ranch, especially to see her.

If Jeffrey managed to find her, why couldn't John find her too? Why had she never seen a trace of John? Why had nobody ever heard his name—John Zumwalt? Where was John? Was he even alive? Hot tears tumbled over Vienna's cheeks.

"Please, God, let my golden hero be alive. Lead me to him and let us be man and wife," she prayed.

The target shooting stopped behind the house. Father, Jeffrey, and Orion ambled around the corner.

"Don't bother to see me off, Mr. Brooks, sir. Save your legs," Jeffrey called.

Father must have been in pain, for he went inside the cabin without a word of protest. When Vienna fetched a bucket of water for Jeffrey's horse, Jeffrey looked pleased.

"Your father taught me a thing or two," he told her. While the horse slurped water, he contemplated her. "You used to put a blanket around my shoulders during rainstorms," he reminded her. "You were good and kind."

"And you used to milk our cow," she said.

"The rain doused our campfire, remember?"

"I felt like crying, but you laughed." Vienna marveled at the memories surfacing in her mind. She giggled. "You brought pine branches and called them the pioneers' mattresses."

"So I did!"

Vienna laughed as they recalled more funny happenings. She wanted to like Jeffrey again, but could she trust him?

"May I come back, Vienna?" he pleaded. "You're the best thing that ever happened to me, and you're pretty. Do you hear me, Vienna Brooks? I want to come back for you."

She cleared her throat. "I'm sorry, Jeffrey, but I met a wonderful young man. I'll wait for him."

"Where does he live?"

Vienna shrugged in misery. "I don't know."

"Think about me, Vienna, for our paths will cross again." Jeffrey climbed into the buggy and urged the horse to speed away.

Chapter Five
Zeke

Vienna climbed the rise to the vegetable garden located a mile from the house. Since Jeffrey's visit the day before, she had been restless and impatient. She felt life was passing her by.

She studied the string beans that clambered over wooden supports, smothered with white blossoms and crisp, tender pods. She scanned the straight rows of carrots and, sighing, set one of the two baskets she was carrying inside the fence the twins had built to keep out wild animals. She'd harvest the vegetables later.

She wanted to get out into the world, to meet people and improve her chances of finding John.

A cow lowed in a pasture high above the river. Vienna looked for the twins. She spotted them lying in the shade of rocky outcroppings. The boys were catching up on sleep while the cows rested under a spreading oak. Protected from the burning rays of the August sun, the animals chewed their cuds and flicked off flies with busy tails.

Elisha sprang up at her approach. "Is that you, sis?"

"It's me." Tenderness overwhelmed her as she hugged

the slender lad. Of all her brothers, she loved and admired Elisha the most. The older of the twins had proven himself a leader, starting in boyhood. Elijah looked to his brother for guidance, letting him decide whether an action was right or wrong. Both were generous and always ready to do a favor for their only sister.

Swallowing the lump that had stolen into her throat, Vienna said, "Mother sends lunch. You must be starved."

Elisha lifted the red checkered cloth Mother had draped over the basket and helped himself to a warm biscuit. As he munched, he studied her. "What's wrong, sis?"

Vienna sighed. "Father still hasn't given me permission to enter academy. It's only two weeks until school starts, and I'm still guessing."

Elisha gave her a comforting pat. "He'll come around."

"I don't know, Elisha. I can't figure him out anymore."

"He'll listen to Mother."

"I hope she'll talk to him, because if she doesn't the money paid for my tuition will be lost."

"Oh, sis, you'll be a student before you know it."

"Thanks, Elisha!" Vienna felt like tousling her brother's smooth, brown hair, but the 14-year-old had gotten too big for that. She hugged him again.

She stood in awe of her brothers. The boys had paid the two years' tuition for her at the girls' academy. It had been Elisha's idea. Learning that room, board, and travel were additional expenses, the twins worked their fingers to the bone to earn the needed money. She got choked up thinking of her brothers' long workdays and the sacrifices they had made for her, rising before sunup and working all day.

She gently nudged the sleeping Elijah. He rubbed his round, brown eyes and yawned. A smile erupted on his face. "Vienna! Have you permission to leave yet?"

"No, Elijah, but I have warm biscuits."

The twins resembled Mother with their oval faces,

brown eyes, and straight noses. Their clothes dangled on skinny frames. Too often they went without food, yet they insisted that she, their only sister, sit in school and study. They knew what studying meant to her. As the future Mrs. Zumwalt, she needed business skills. John's plan was to earn his livelihood as a storekeeper. John supported his widowed mother and younger brother, and once he got married there'd also be children to bring up properly. John expected his wife to excel. Vienna frowned. She was rusty in English and math, and she knew nothing about the fancy subjects offered at the academy.

She sat awhile and chatted with her brothers. The boys loved company. Blue jays chased and scolded one another in tree branches near the Feather River. The river was low, the pasture brown. No rain had fallen all summer, and the snowmelt of the previous spring had spent itself. With concern, she noticed the cows' small udders. Two calves were due in the rainy season, when fresh green grass sprouted in the foothills. Vienna hoped her family could subsist until the two cows gave milk again.

Troubled, she picked up the lunch basket and left. Back at the garden, she yanked carrots from the warm soil and fitted them into the baskets on a bed of greens. Then she heaped both baskets with string beans.

Just as she was ready to lug her load home, she heard approaching hoofbeats. Zeke, the gold miner, popped up at the fence. The big fellow looked like a giant on his little donkey. He had been coming around a lot lately, she realized. He doffed his crumpled hat to her. The hat had smashed down his brown hair, leaving sweaty beads on his forehead. His gray, good-natured eyes looked friendly under his sloping brows.

"Let Jack carry those baskets," he offered.

"Thanks, but I can manage." Vienna smiled up at the pudgy face sporting a shiny, sunburned nose. She liked the gold miner even though he smelled a little rank, if one was downwind. Zeke was a comfortable sort. There wasn't a mean bone in his body, she guessed. His wide, upturned mouth belied the fact he was mourning his mother, who had died back East in his absence. Elisha reported that Zeke had sobbed like a baby on receiving the sad news from the States.

"You looked very pretty on the Sabbath," he said. "It's always a joy to see you at church. You're clean and respectful, just like my ma."

"I'm sorry about your mother, Zeke. I'm sure God gave her the best place."

He brightened. "God bless you, Miss Vienna."

Vienna set the baskets outside the fence and closed the gate. "Excuse me, Zeke. I must get home."

Zeke cleared his throat. "There's somethin' I've been meanin' to ask you."

"Yes, Zeke?"

"I've been meanin' to tell you at church every week." His face flushed.

"Tell me what?"

"I asked your brother, the one who calls himself Elisha, if I kin come and meet your folks, and now I'm askin' you." He chewed his words without hurry. "It's on account of . . ."

The dimples in his pudgy cheeks vanished. His eyes compressed. He loosened his bandanna, then crushed and pinched and rolled his hat. "It's 'cause I'd like to come courtin'. Would you marry me and be my darlin' wife?"

Vienna gasped.

"Afore you say no, Miss Vienna, I'm a God-fearin' man. I kin support a wife and family. I'd be right proud to take care of you."

Vienna wiped perspiration from her forehead. She felt sorry for the miner. "You're a good person, Zeke, and I appreciate all you're trying to do for me. You never miss Sabbath services, and you've been very kind to Elisha."

"A fine boy, that one."

She nodded. "Elisha told me about your good luck. People say you're a rich man, Zeke. That puts you ahead of others, I suppose."

"God gave me gold, Miss Vienna, but without a wife I'm still a poor sucker."

"Oh, Zeke, I know you'll find a good wife. As for me, I'm spoken for."

His face fell. "Who is he? I never see him around."

"His name is John, and I don't know where he is. You see, we met three years ago. I last saw him somewhere in the Rocky Mountains."

He brightened. "Ain't no man gonna wait three years for a woman."

Something snapped inside Vienna. "Go, Zeke! Don't come around again. Leave!" She marched home, leaving miner and donkey behind. John had promised he'd wait for her if it took half a dozen years.

The blond girl on the wagon train popped into Vienna's mind. Supposing . . .

"You're silly, Vienna Brooks," she told herself firmly. "John is good and true."

At home she hoisted her baskets onto the table. Father left his woodworking job in the lean-to. His crutches thumped on the threshold. "What kept you so long?" he barked.

"Am I late, Pa?"

"Did that miner on the jackass come around again?"

Vienna felt taken aback. "If you mean Zeke, yes, he did stop by. He asked me to marry him, Pa."

"What did you tell him?"

"That I will wait for John." Vienna turned and ran out of the house. She didn't know what to make of her father's bad mood. He must be in pain, she concluded.

She wrested clothes and diapers from the line. The fresh, outdoorsy smell reminded her of John. She felt miserable. As she folded the wash she mentally composed a letter to her childhood friend, Priscilla. She never bothered to write her confessions down or send them off anymore. In her unwritten letters she confided her true feelings.

"My life is a mess, Priss. No letter from you, ever. No trace of John. No permission to enter academy. To top it all, Pa is angry with me."

Chapter Six
Father Decides

The afternoon breeze carried the scent of pines. Vienna inhaled the good smell as she listened to miners' voices echoing from canyon walls. A hen emerged from her nest, cackling triumphantly, and a squirrel struck droll poses on an overhead bough. Vienna thought life couldn't get more peaceful; still she felt restless.

Since Zeke's visit at the garden two days earlier, she and Mother had been sewing clothes. Vienna swatted at a pesky mosquito, squashing the insect before it bit her cheek. Mother looked up.

"Put on more salve, daughter. You don't want to arrive at school with a blemished face."

Vienna forced a laugh. "I will, Mother."

"What's so funny, daughter?"

"If Pa doesn't let me go I can show off my new clothes right here in Bidwell Bar."

Mother was sewing a crocheted collar to Vienna's pink travel dress. "Your father will change his mind about your leaving, daughter. He will do what's best for you." Mother's mouth curved upward in an encouraging smile.

"I hope you're right, Mother. I wish I had your confidence." Vienna reached for the ointment jar Mother kept close at hand. She spread the clinging salve over her cheeks, then wiped her hands on a rag. "You want some too, Mother?"

Mother shook her head. "When you get to the academy, daughter, I hope you will consider preparing yourself for the career of a teacher. Teaching children is a privilege and a duty." Mother reached down and tousled baby Jay's curly blond hair. The toddler was playing contentedly with scraps from Father's workshop.

"You had lots of schooling, Mother," Vienna reflected. "Me? I'm just an ignorant farm girl."

"Not so, daughter! Remember that you will be an educated young lady two years hence." Mother moistened the end of her thread before pulling it through the needle's eye. "I hope your teachers can offer the high quality of instruction I received in my home state of Connecticut."

"Why don't you come and judge for yourself, Mother? We could travel together. It would do you good to get out into the world for a change."

"We have no extra money, daughter, and who would look after little Jay? Who would look after your father? You must travel alone, I fear." Mother sighed.

"You love to travel, Mother. Isn't there any way you can come with me?"

"It is true. I love new horizons, but travel is expensive. Besides, who would nurse your father should he get sick?"

"If Pa lets me go I'll record everything I see and tell you about it," Vienna promised.

Mother's mouth curved in a mischievous smile. Eyes dancing with fun, she said, "You can always trust a Scholfield to come through for you."

"I will do your family proud, Mother. I will study hard, provided Pa lets me go."

"He will." Mother snipped off the thread. "Always remember that you are a Scholfield, a member of my family, daughter. Scholfields demand the highest and best of themselves, knowing that God deserves the very best one has to give. In the New England tradition, they believe in thrift, integrity, and individuality."

"What if I make mistakes, Mother? What if I cannot live up to their example?"

"Mistakes will teach you to do better next time. Learn from your mistakes, daughter. Avoid repeating them."

"What if others talk me into doing something I don't want to do? You know how I hate disagreements."

"Don't listen to them, daughter. Always listen to your own conscience."

Vienna fidgeted. Mother could get so serious. "Why don't you get any letters from your family?" she prodded. "Why don't they write?"

Mother held up Vienna's dress. She appeared pleased with the fine and even stitches she had made. Sunbeams caught in her light brown hair, creating golden highlights. Eyes sparkling, she explained. "I was a young girl when I left my family and the woolen mill they owned. Your father swept into my life like a whirlwind, Vienna. We pioneered, first in Ohio, then in Michigan. Country life was fun for me, a city girl, though the work was hard."

"What was pioneering like in those days?"

"Same as today in 1855," Mother laughed. "We cleared the forest, started a farm, raised a roof."

"What about the Scholfields? Why don't they write?"

"In the backwoods where you children were born, postal service was either absent or unreliable." Mother's fine brows drew together. "We lost contact."

"Couldn't you let your family know where we live now?"

Mother drew a deep breath. She reached for the bodice of a dress and started to sew on a button. "I shall attempt to contact my older brother, Albert Gallatin."

"When, Mother?"

"When you become a teacher, Vienna. Albert and I used to sit by the fire sometimes. He told me of his desire to start a business college in our hometown of Jewett City. Albert will be delighted to know that my only daughter aspires to become a teacher."

Vienna fingered the hem she was basting, marshaling her courage. "My true plan is to marry John."

Mother's nimble fingers pushed the needle through the cotton material. Had Mother heard her? Vienna spoke louder. "John will want me to work in his store, Mother. My future is decided."

Mother gave Vienna her most penetrating gaze. "If John rode up this minute, would you follow him?"

"Oh, yes, Mother!"

"Three full years have passed since you last saw John. Are you certain he is the one and only man you will ever want?"

"He is, Mother!"

"The most capable girl can ruin her life by marrying the wrong man, daughter. The wrong decision can make her suffer forever. Marriage is a lifelong commitment."

"Oh, Mother! John is definitely the right man for me. I can feel it in my heart."

"You may be living a dream, daughter." Mother's gaze still rested on Vienna. "Surely, John believes we perished in the wilderness. Ours was the last wagon to cross the Sierra Nevada in 1852. If your father had not found us at the last moment we would have perished."

"But we made it, Mother. We're alive!"

"Does John know that?"

Teardrops fell on Vienna's unfinished dress. "John is waiting for me, Mother. I can feel it."

The next morning Mother went into town for supplies. "No need to expect me for lunch, daughter. I shall stop and see the twins on my way back."

After she left, Father went back to bed. Vienna stepped to his side. "Is anything wrong, Father?"

"My head," Father groaned. He was shaking. "Cover me, Vienna. I'm freezing."

Vienna gathered covers and bundled him up. She hurriedly brewed the herbal tea Mother kept for emergencies. He sipped it slowly, a little at a time. Vienna sat by his side, alert to his every move. When he tossed off the covers, she quickly dipped strips of cloth into the water bucket and placed them on his forehead, arms, and chest. She kept renewing the cloth strips, trying to bring his temperature down. By now he was babbling.

Vienna leaned over him. "Can I get you something, Pa?"

"My baby Vienna."

She swallowed. He was using a tone of voice she hadn't heard in ages.

"You're my good little girl. Do you want your pa to put you on the pony? Do you want to play on the swing?"

In desperation Vienna said, "I am growing up, Pa. I'm no longer a baby."

"You'll never leave your pa, will you? Not my little baby Vienna."

"I need to think of my future," Vienna sobbed. "Please let me go, Pa!" Then she scolded herself for speaking out of turn to a sick man.

He broke out in a sweat, drenching the bedding. Vienna attempted to make him comfortable. At the end of his fever attack, Father appeared exhausted and fell asleep.

Orion and Elmont stepped to the bed, solemn-faced. "Is he dead?" they asked.

Vienna stemmed her panic. "Your father is fine," she assured the boys. "Go collect the eggs. Feed the chickens. Fill the wood box. Do it without making any noise. We mustn't wake Pa."

The boys obeyed.

Father dead?

She posted herself at the door. What was keeping Mother? A ground squirrel sounded alarm, and its charges flipped into holes. The sentinel had spotted Mother as she neared the cabin with her purposeful stride. Mother resembled a cheerful young girl with her arms filled with baskets.

"Elisha needed rips mended and buttons sewed on," Mother laughed. "You know what a lively lad the boy is. We enjoyed a great visit. There are a thousand things Elisha wants to know." She paused. "You look shaken, daughter. Is anything wrong?"

Vienna pointed to the bed. "Pa suffered one of his fever attacks."

"The poor man!" Mother set down the baskets and rushed to his side.

Father was up and very quiet the next day. Mother said she'd wait until he felt stronger before bringing up Vienna's problem.

"It's now or never, Mother!" Vienna urged in desperation.

Mother gave in at long last. "We must give our daughter permission to leave," she told Father. "The school year is about to commence, and she mustn't arrive late. Our daughter has a good head on her shoulders. She can learn and make us proud."

"But will she be safe?" Father asked. "Will she be protected from those young swains who chase after innocent girls?"

Mother fetched the academy's guidebook. She opened it to a well-worn page and enunciated in her most crisp and distinct manner. "Young ladies will not be allowed to walk or ride out unless in company with one of their parents or teachers. Pupils cannot receive calls from any persons except those introduced by the parents or guardians to the principal or governess. Passing the vicinity of a gambling house or saloon is forbidden. There will be no excursions on the Sabbath. Sabbath is strictly observed."

Father stroked his beard. "Will these standards be enforced, you think?"

"Absolutely! The school's reputation depends on it, dearest."

"Maybe she'll be safer there than here." Father's head jerked up as a donkey brayed outside. He reached for his crutches and moved himself to the door. Tearing the door ajar, he shook a crutch at the donkey and its rider. Then, face flushed, he slammed the door shut.

"It's that gold miner again!" Father's arm made a stabbing motion toward the guidebook. "It's decided; our daughter will attend academy."

Vienna stopped stirring the soup over the fire and flew into her father's arms. "Thank you, Pa! I'll always love you for this."

Chapter Seven
Old Reliable

The September day promised to dawn brighter than any Vienna remembered. Predawn breezes carried the scent of dewy pines. Ducks winged south, punctuating the air with their noisy cries. Vienna set her bag, packed the day before, outside the cabin door. She inhaled and smiled. She also was traveling south. She reopened her bag, wondering if she'd forgotten anything important.

Inside the cabin, Mother hoisted a pot of oatmeal onto the table. "Come and eat breakfast, daughter," she called.

Vienna reached down to the bottom of the bag, feeling for her moccasins. "I guess I did pack everything, Mother." Satisfied, she went inside.

Candlelight flickered on the table, and her parents' faces looked ghostly in the uncertain light. Father ladled his oatmeal listlessly.

Vienna blew over the steaming food. She wasn't hungry and barely managed to empty her bowl.

Mother looked concerned. "Eat, daughter! It will be a while until you get another meal. You have a long day of travel ahead of you. The eggs and biscuits in your bag won't last forever."

"I'm too excited, Mother. I've never left home before." Vienna fidgeted, wondering what she'd do if she missed the stage or riverboat. She waited until her parents finished eating, then cleared the table.

Mother fastened a fine brooch to the collar of her dress. The brooch had been a gift from Grandmother Scholfield.

"But Mother, you've worn the brooch only for church," Vienna exclaimed.

Mother nodded. "It is true; I wear this heirloom for divine services. I am wearing it today because this marks an important milestone in our lives, and we beg the Lord's blessing. Starting today, life will change for all of us."

Vienna couldn't miss the solemn tone in Mother's voice. She didn't know what to say. Through the open door she watched the twins harness the ponies to the wagon. She checked on baby Jay, still sleeping soundly in his trundle bed. Vienna kissed his soft cheek, then pulled up his cover.

Noises grew loud in the loft as Orion and Elmont scrambled out of the straw.

"What's going on?" Orion demanded, climbing down the ladder.

"Why is it dark?" Elmont piped.

Mother grasped the 7-year-old's hand and spoke gently. "We are going on a trip, Elmont. Do you wish to come along?"

"Will there be big, bad men, Mother?"

"No, Elmont, but we may pass some horseback riders and miners on foot. They will not hurt you, son."

"I'm not going! I'm scared." Elmont scrambled back up the ladder.

Mother turned to Orion. "Will you look after your brothers, son? We shan't be long."

Orion's lower lip trembled. "Can I come along to see Vienna off?"

"No, son. Somebody must stay with Jay and Elmont."

About to follow the twins to the wagon, Vienna turned back. She felt hot and muddled inside. Orion had always been her special charge. In a flush of emotion she bent down and squeezed the 9-year-old boy.

"It's all right, Orion. We'll say goodbye right here."

"Don't go away, Vienna! Please stay!" Orion's clear blue eyes reddened with tears.

Vienna's innards lurched. "I'm not leaving, Mother," she declared. "It's selfish of me to go off and abandon my duties."

Mother lifted Orion's chin. "You are a big boy and a leader, son. Leaders don't cry."

Orion sniffled. "Sorry, Mother."

"Do you want Vienna to be happy, son?"

"Yes, Mother." Orion's fists rubbed away salty tears.

"I shall give you a special honor, son," Mother promised. "I shall put you in charge of your brothers."

"Thank you, Mother," Orion beamed.

Mother turned to Vienna. "We can manage without you, daughter. This is no time to change your mind. You must prepare for your future. Without education you will be only half the person you can be. God gave us talents, so we must develop them."

"I feel so selfish, Mother."

"No, Vienna. Learning to serve the common good is never selfish."

Vienna hung her head. "Sorry, Mother." Mother was referring to teaching.

The twins poked their heads into the cabin. "Hurry up; the stage won't wait!" they urged.

Elisha assisted Father to the wagon. Elijah grabbed Vienna's bag and tossed it behind the seat.

Careful not to trip over the hem of her new dress, Vienna boosted herself onto the wagon and sat next to Father. Mother mounted to her right, and the twins jumped on in back. Vienna inhaled the bracing air and waited for the sun to rise.

"Whoa!" Father set the brake at the stage stop. Getting off the wagon with Elisha's help, he exclaimed, "That's it! Our little Vienna is flying the coop."

"I'll be back for next year's summer vacation, Pa. Time will pass quickly; you'll see!"

She jumped from the wagon behind Mother. The stage-coach, harnessed to a team of snorting horses, stood ready. The driver climbed down from his high seat and opened the rear boot. The boys tossed in Vienna's bag, then faced her with sheepish expressions.

Vienna pumped her brothers' hands. "Thank you for everything." Choked with emotion, she drew Elisha aside and whispered, "If you see John, please tell him where I am."

Elisha nodded vigorously.

"It's time, Miss," the driver urged.

Vienna threw herself around Mother's neck. "Goodbye, Mother."

Mother held her tight. "You will have learned teachers, daughter. I expect you to obey them." Mother's eyes swam, and Vienna's cheeks felt hot.

"What about me?" Father joked. "Don't I get a hug?"

Vienna embraced Father, careful not to unbalance his crutches. His beard pricked her face. Elisha assisted her into the coach and closed the door behind her.

"Don't worry about a thing, sis," he said.

In the dawn's gray light, she sat down opposite a miner who appeared to be sleeping, his hat covering his eyes and face. *A weary traveler,* she thought. Relieved that she didn't have to wedge herself between strangers, she waved to her family.

"'Bye, Mother! 'Bye, Pa! 'Bye, Elisha! 'Bye, Elijah!'" Vienna's handkerchief fluttered until her family vanished from sight.

Settling into the window seat, she yawned. The coach's rocking motions made her sleepy. She leaned against the headrest, meaning to catch up on sleep. The day promised to be long, and she planned to arrive fresh and rested.

Suddenly her eyelids flew open. The miner across from her had flipped off his hat and was grinning.

"Zeke, is that you?" she cried. "What are you doing here?"

"You didn't think I'd let you travel alone, did you?"

"You are too much, Zeke! If my father knew you were traveling with me he'd yank me off this coach."

"If your pa knew, he'd thank me for lookin' out after you, Miss Vienna." Zeke moved to her side.

Vienna bristled. She sensed the heat of his body and the moist breath coming from his mouth. "What are you doing?" she asked.

"The best seat inside a stage is the one next to the driver, Miss Vienna. You get less jostlin'. I saved it 'specially for you." He pointed to the seat he had just vacated.

Vienna scooted away from him. The seat was warm and smelled just a bit rank. Avoiding looking at him directly, she scanned the brightening landscape. Her stomach felt queasy, and her head felt strange.

Zeke grinned. "You'll get used to ridin' backwards, Miss Vienna. Hang on."

He gave more directions. "When the whip—I mean, the driver—asks you to get off and walk, do it without grumblin'. He won't ask unless it's necessary."

"What if the horses run away?"

"Sit still and hang on. If you jump, you'll get hurt." Zeke paused, apparently waiting for a comment.

She remained silent.

"Ain't you glad you're not sittin' with a smoker?" he asked.

Vienna sighed.

"Ain't you glad you're not sittin' with folks who pass the whiskey bottle?" he challenged.

"I loathe whiskey."

"Ain't you glad you're not sittin' with folks who point out every murder scene they pass?"

She didn't answer.

If we get into a holdup, you'll be safe," he assured her. "The feller who rides beside the whip isn't called shotgun for nothin'. He'll protect you with his gun, and I'll protect you with my fists. I'd give my life to keep you from harm, Miss Vienna." He spoke kindly, as if speaking to a child.

Vienna peeled the shawl from her shoulders. Zeke promptly rolled down the canvas curtains on one side, shutting out the glorious morning sun.

"Your face is gettin' red," he observed.

"I am fine, Zeke."

Vienna fanned herself. The way things were going, she wouldn't get much rest on the coach. Having missed sleep the night before, she felt tired and on edge. She yearned for more sleep.

As the sun warmed, Zeke fanned her face with the crumpled brim of his hat. "Is that better, Miss Vienna?"

"Yes, thank you, Zeke."

"Kin I take off your shoes, Miss Vienna?"

"No, thank you, Zeke."

He tossed his hat onto the seat. "Ain't you glad we're not sittin' with folks who swear?"

"Yes, Zeke."

"Ain't you glad we're not sittin' with folks who chew tobacco and spit out the window?"

"Yes, Zeke."

Vienna's chest heaved. How much longer did she have to endure Zeke's fawning? He needed a shave. He must have headed for the stagecoach at the crack of dawn. "Where did you leave your donkey?" she asked.

"Jack's in the stable."

"Why don't you turn back and keep Jack company?" Vienna suggested. "I'm sure he misses you."

"Jack's gotta wait until I've dropped you off at the school where you're goin'."

Vienna gulped. "You want to accompany me all the way to San Francisco Bay?"

"Wouldn't have it no other way." Dimples appeared in his ruddy cheeks. "I'll bed me down in a haymow tonight and travel back tomorrow." He leaned back happily without a worry in the world.

At the Marysville ferry landing, Zeke hustled her to the departing riverboat. Banners fluttered above the passengers boarding the vessel. Vienna wanted to look for John, but Zeke kept her distracted. The boiler made a racket, the smoke stacks belched out black smoke, and the calliope whistle shrilled. They pushed off and chugged down the Feather River.

Vienna wanted to walk about, but she couldn't. Zeke steered her to a crowded bench along the railing. When he turned to walk away, she saw the tails of his red flannel shirt hanging out and the hair curling down into his shirt collar.

"Where are you going?" Vienna called.

"To get you somethin' to drink."

He returned, smiling good-naturedly, clasping a tin cup. "Drink!" he ordered.

She sipped cool river water and handed back the cup. "Thank you, Zeke."

He went off again, returning with bread and a slice of cheese. "Eat!"

Vienna nibbled. "Thank you, Zeke."

"You're gettin' mighty red," he fretted as the sun climbed higher.

"I am all right, Zeke."

He pulled the bandanna off his neck and fashioned it into some sort of tent. Holding it over her head, he asked, "Is this better, Miss Vienna?"

"I am all right, Zeke."

Vienna yearned to look for John. She had looked forward to savoring this day, planning to mentally prepare herself for the academy. Instead, she felt smothered.

"Kin I bring you somethin' else, Miss Vienna?" Zeke asked in his easygoing way.

"No, Zeke," Vienna snapped. "Why are you fussing over me?"

He patted her arm. "Think of me as Old Reliable, Miss Vienna. Calm down and you'll be fine."

Chapter Eight
"Miss Graham"

Vienna left Zeke at the door of the academy, where he had identified himself as her "brother." She arrived after dark, later than she had expected. Registration was still going on, though, because other girls also arrived late.

The school smelled of paint and wood stain. Carpenters hammered away in the registration area, putting on finishing touches. The newly built school was located on land that had belonged, until recently, to a Spanish family.

"I hope you're not too hungry. The dining room closed an hour ago," the clerk apologized as she handed Vienna her registration papers.

"I have a snack in my bag," Vienna said, feeling more hot than hungry.

The janitor escorted her upstairs. He set her bag inside a dormitory room and hurried off. Vienna set the candle she was given on a small desk. The room was stuffy. She pulled back the curtain and opened the window. Marine air, salty and sharp, stung her face. Shivering, she shrugged into her woolen shawl. As far as she could tell in the uncertain light, the window overlooked a bare yard, bordered by a white picket fence.

Turning around, she frowned at four bunk beds along the room's two long walls. Was she going to share her room with three other girls? The idea gave her goose bumps. An odd taste crept into Vienna's mouth. She regretted coming to this place.

"I ought to have listened to you, Father," she muttered. "I could sleep at home."

She put her few possessions into an armoire and a chest of drawers, leaving room for the other girls. Sitting by the tiny desk on the room's only chair, she removed her shoes and slipped into her moccasins, adjusting the rawhide lacing.

"Ah!" she sighed with pleasure.

The moccasins were old. Though darker than when she first got them on the westward trail, they nevertheless showed character. Somehow they had grown and stretched with her feet over the years. They hugged her feet softly like a second skin. The face of the Indian woman who had sewn the moccasins surfaced in Vienna's mind. Twinkling blood-shot eyes, leathery skin tanned by the merciless prairie sun, veined dark hands that carried sinew to worn-down teeth wet with saliva . . . It all came back to her. Memories of the adorable Indian children who clung shyly to their mother. And other memories came unbidden.

Vienna reached down to the bottom of her bag. She withdrew the new diary Mother had given her as a parting gift. From its pristine pages, she withdrew the rosebud John had given her during the unforgettable stop at the Platte River. Inhaling its lingering scent, she remembered shimmering waters, dappled sunshine, and John.

"You're like this rosebud," John had told her. "I'll wait for you if it takes half a dozen years."

Vienna eased the fragile rosebud back between the pages and put the diary under her pillow. She spread her flannel gown on top of the bed, wondering if she should wait up for the other girls. Finally feeling hungry, she savored one of Mother's boiled eggs.

At the next day's welcoming ceremony, half the seats in the auditorium gaped empty. Vienna, who had spent the night alone, listened to directions given by the governess. Dutifully, she scribbled down rules and regulations so she could refer to them later. Her pencil was scratching away when a stir distracted the speaker.

A redhead in a stylish green outfit was making a late entrance. The governess paused as the girl picked her way to a center seat up front.

Is she my roommate? Vienna wondered. The information sheet on her lap listed "Miss Brooks" and "Miss Graham" next to her room number.

The governess ended her talk. The principal, a clergyman who also was listed as professor of moral philosophy, mounted the dais. He launched into his talk without formalities.

"All through the annals of our race, from Adam down to Washington, the sad story runs of the neglect and degradation of women.

"Women, the natural conservators of the higher virtues in the world, were made into hewers of wood and drawers of water, shrouded into veils, and compelled to hobble in narrow, unyielding shoes.

"It is woman who trains the child from infancy to maturity, at home and in school, and if you limit her education, you have a blind leader of the blind. The Bible and common sense tell you what becomes of both. Woman is the exponent of the moral tone, the integrity, the fiber, the virtue of the state, but it has taken a long time for the world to learn that she can measure her intellect with that of her brother.

"In our primary schools back East, the girls carry off most of the prizes. In our high schools, they average up to their brothers. In our academies and colleges, they hold their own." He looked around, challenging each student.

"I welcome you to the Alameda Institute, Academy of Girls, and congratulate you on choosing education. Owing to girls like you, we can look with confidence to an enlightened and virtuous society."

Vienna scribbled like mad, wishing Mother could hear the principal's inspiring speech.

Entering her room later on, Vienna stumbled over fancy bags smelling of lavender. The redhead in the green outfit stood at the window. She whirled around.

"Miss Brooks? Vienna Brooks?"

"Why, yes."

"Is it really you, Vienna? I'm Priscilla! Don't you recognize me?"

"But—your name is Graham!"

Vienna scrutinized the girl. She was delicate and short, with well-groomed hair, alabaster skin, and wore a lacy jabot fastened to an elegant bodice by a golden filigree brooch. This couldn't be Priss, her Michigan backwoods friend! And yet the mischievous green eyes, the pixie smile, and the freckles spelled PRISCILLA in capital letters.

"Priss!" Vienna cried. "It is you!"

As the girls embraced, sudden tears tumbled over Vienna's cheeks.

"Why didn't you write? Why didn't you answer my letters?" Vienna asked.

Priscilla drew back. "What letters? I never got any."

"You didn't?"

"No! My family headed West in the spring of 1853, a year after you departed. There simply wasn't enough time for a letter to reach me, I guess."

"I wrote to you before we struck out into Indian country. Mother posted the letter."

"I didn't get it."

Vienna dried her tears, feeling foolish. "I never considered this possibility. How was your overland journey, Priss? Did you have a rough time?"

"It was dreadful, I tell you." Priscilla shook herself. "Terrible water, sick people, awful food, and always the fear of Indian attacks. I wouldn't repeat that journey for anything. What's even worse"—Priscilla dabbed a lacy handkerchief at reddening eyelids—"Pa picked a quarrel with a teamster and got himself killed in a stupid gunfight. You know what a hothead Pa was."

"I'm so sorry, Priss." Vienna squeezed her friend in sympathy. "How did your ma get along?"

"Fine. She married the nice widower who helped Phil drive our wagon over the Sierra."

"You have a stepfather?"

"He's the greatest, Vienna. He loves Mother, and he adopted me."

"What about your brother?"

"Phil is too old for adoption. Besides, he's still grieving over Pa."

"I am so sorry." Vienna tried to digest Priscilla's news.

"What about you? How did you fare?" Priscilla asked.

"We were fortunate, Priss. All of us are alive—Mother, Father, and all my brothers. We're in the milk business, up north in Butte County."

"Who brought you here?"

"I, uh, traveled alone. There was no extra travel money."

"No money?" Priscilla looked surprised. "Daddy is a banker; he has lots of money. Mother and Phil brought me up from the city, that's San Francisco, of course."

"You live in San Francisco?"

"It's where Daddy conducts his banking business."

Vienna's head whirled. "What subjects are you taking?" She couldn't think of anything else to say.

"Mother insisted I take music with the use of the piano."

"That's an extra $50 a year, Priss!" Vienna gasped. "Why, that's the entire cost of my tuition for two years!"

"No matter," Priscilla shrugged. "Mother also enrolled me in ornamental branches—French embroidery, Oriental painting, and wax flower creations."

Vienna gulped. "That's another $15 a year."

"Daddy doesn't mind. He's got the money. How about you? Are you taking only basic subjects?"

Vienna nodded with conviction. "That's what I need— English and math, especially math."

Priscilla tugged at the cascading ruffles at her throat. "Basic subjects include domestic economy. I'm taking that too." She studied the narrow room. "Where can I put my things?"

Vienna went to the armoire. "Here, for starters. I left room for you and the two other girls."

Priscilla frowned. "How am I going to get all my stuff in there?"

"I left room for you in this chest of drawers too, see?" Vienna pulled out a drawer. Her things lay neatly at one side.

"What about the other girls? Where will they put their things?" Priscilla asked.

"You better leave room for them."

"Ridiculous! I'll be lucky if I get my stuff in here at all." Priscilla opened her bags and emptied the contents onto the bed across from the one Vienna had chosen.

"Don't work yourself into a temper tantrum, Priss. We're here, and we're lucky to learn something."

Priscilla's upturned little nose wrinkled. "Maybe you're lucky. This is pretty tough for me, you know. I have my own room in San Francisco. I'm not used to sharing."

Chapter Nine
Phil

Vienna heard a commotion down the hall. In the three weeks since her arrival at the school, she hadn't heard anything so crude. She pulled the door ajar. Screams mingled with the high-pitched voice of the governess, as she helped the janitor drag along a loudly protesting girl.

"You won't get me in this jail. Let me go!"

The struggling party moved toward Vienna, who yielded before the ragamuffin girl who was wearing men's clothing.

"You won't get me in here! I won't have it!" the girl screamed.

The governess yanked the girl into the room, then straightened her dress. "You will introduce yourself without fail," she commanded.

"No, I won't!" The girl kicked the governess's shin and snapped at the janitor.

"This is Miss Molly Steele." Face distorted with pain, the governess made a formal introduction. "These are your roommates," she told the girl. "Miss Priscilla Graham and Miss Vienna Brooks." Collecting herself, the governess added, "We shall have you fitted for clothes tomorrow. You will not attend classes until you are properly attired."

"I don't care about your classes. And I don't want your clothes!" Molly spit at her.

The governess wiped Molly's spittle from her face, struggling for composure. "You will do as I say, Molly Steele. We have your parents' orders to change you into a civilized young lady." The governess gave the janitor a signal, and both left the room.

Molly tore the door open and spit at the janitor, who remained outside in the hall. "She left him at the door," Molly complained. "I'm in a prison, and he's guarding me." She plunked herself onto the chair. Pulling at her unkempt blond hair, she stared at her roommates and sneered, "Prim and Prissy! I might have known!"

Priscilla looked the newcomer over as if she were some exotic creature. "Where do you come from?"

"San Francisco."

"Is your father rich?"

"Of course, he's rich. He's an importer. That's why she married him, that fine lady who stepped off the boat with her steamer trunks. She pestered Pa until he committed me to this place. She says I need polish. Huh!"

"What's your father's name?" Priscilla probed.

"Steele. The old governess dragon just told you."

"What does your father import?"

"Chilean flour, barrels of beef, rolls of sheet lead, tons of wire, bales of goods, whiskey, and tobacco. Why?"

Priscilla fluttered a hand. "Just wanted to know if you're real."

"Of course I'm real!" Molly spit onto the floor.

Priscilla turned her head to one side and put on her pixie smile. "Have you heard of the banker, Mr. Graham?"

"Everybody has. Pa does business with him."

Priscilla extended her hand. "I am his daughter. Welcome! We'll get along fine."

Vienna gasped. She thought Priscilla would complain. Instead, her friend was playing the charmer. She had objected to Fran, the girl whose wheezing and coughing got on her nerves, and despite Fran's earnest pleading, Priscilla made her pack up and move. Vienna still felt sorry for Fran; the girl had been neat, and she appeared helpless.

Molly was 2 years older than Vienna and Priscilla, but they shared some of the same classes. Once Molly relaxed in her newly fitted dress, she shattered the air with explosive laughter. The first time Vienna heard the cackling laugh, she froze. Molly was, without doubt, the girl who had flirted with John—and who had met John's mother.

Even so, Molly's laugh proved infectious. Molly could laugh and laugh, finding the smallest happenings humorous. She had been repulsive to Vienna at first. Her loud voice, her coarseness, and her blunt questions shocked and annoyed Vienna. Molly was a creature unlike any she had known, yet there was something refreshing about the uninhibited girl.

Molly took one of the upper beds. The fourth bed was still empty, and the three girls wondered whether or not another roommate was coming. With October rains threatening to muddy the roads, they rather doubted it.

A violent storm came in mid-October. Rain prattled against classroom windows and wind screamed around house corners, distracting students and teachers alike.

Priscilla loathed the storm. "If this keeps up, Mother and Phil can't come to see me," she pouted.

Weeks of sunshine followed the three-day storm and dried out the roads. Mrs. Graham arrived in a carriage her banker husband kept at the ferry landing. As a parent she was allowed to take her daughter outside.

Thanks to Priscilla's prodding, Vienna received permission to come along. An elegant lady sat in the back seat as the governess escorted Vienna to the carriage.

"You will be responsible for your daughter's friend," the governess impressed upon the lady.

"The girl will be fine," Mrs. Graham promised.

Vienna felt at ease seeing Priscilla's mother and

smelling her familiar lavender scent. The former Mrs. Wilson was a charming and pleasant woman. Vienna remembered her as a person who had always been nice and who never seemed to worry about a thing. Her figure had become rounder, though, and the voice sounded softer. The strawberry hair showed silver streaks, and her formerly tanned skin resembled the fine bone china that graced the academy's tables during teatime. Spurning the sunbonnet she used to wear on the farm, the new Mrs. Graham was holding aloft a Chinese umbrella.

"Thank you for taking me along!" Vienna beamed at the woman she'd known since childhood.

Mrs. Graham laughed her comfortable laugh. "What a surprise to find you here, Vienna Brooks!" she said, brown eyes gleaming. "You certainly have grown tall and pretty." Gathering her skirts to make room for Priscilla, she pointed to the driver's seat. "You remember Phil, don't you?"

Vienna gasped as the driver turned around. The awkward youngster whose sleeves and pant legs always rode up would never be overlooked in a crowd now. Wearing a suit, top hat, and cravat, he looked strikingly attractive. She climbed up to sit beside him. "Do you remember me, Phil?"

His violet eyes flashed under the thick black brows beneath the brim of his hat. A mustache extended pointed ends to jet-black sideburns that separated his face and ears like slender peninsulas. Two upper teeth gleamed through the fancy black mustache. Vienna wondered if he was smiling. And was he using his mother's lavender water? Phil used to be his mother's favorite, she remembered.

"Phil, do you remember me?" she asked again.

He nodded. "Vienna," he said, and never addressed her again, though he kept giving her sidelong glances.

On the high seat, with the sea breeze tugging at her sunbonnet, Vienna felt the world was showing her new wonders. She glimpsed San Francisco Bay to the west and, farther north, the strait called Golden Gate that connected the Bay with the Pacific Ocean. Ships sailed in and out, white sails painting jolly patterns on the blue water. To the east, hills rose from the coastal plain.

Where is John? she asked herself. Most emigrant trains entered California over the high pass named after the ill-fated Donner Party. Upon descending the Sierra Nevada, most wagons stopped in the vicinity of Sutter's Fort (an area now known as the city of Sacramento, capital of California since 1854). From Sacramento the emigrants fanned out in several directions. Which way did John go? Did he travel by wagon or by ferry? Where did he wind up?

Supposing he settled in San Francisco! Shivers ran down Vienna's spine. Supposing John settled in that windy, wicked place! *No,* she told herself, *John would never throw himself into the midst of wickedness. John is a God-fearing man. He'd want to shield his younger brother and dear old mother from evil. He'd want his children to grow up in wholesome surroundings.*

Grappling with her thoughts, Vienna fell silent, like Phil beside her. His frequent sidelong glances made her uncomfortable. She concentrated on the names of mercantile houses they passed. John had planned to name his store The BIG Z.

"Whoa!" Phil pulled back on the reins.

A donkey sat on its haunches in the middle of the street. Head thrown back, it screamed, "Hee-haw! Hee-haw!" A miner, who looked a lot like Zeke, pushed the donkey from behind. A gold miner's outfit clattered off the animal's back, making a racket. Pick, shovel, bucket, frying pan, dipper, and iron pot, as well as tin cups, plates, knife, fork, and spoon in canvas bags tumbled to the ground.

The din sent little boys running. Gleefully, they cheered on the donkey's owner. "Get him up! Get him up!"

The miner grasped the reins and flicked them over the animal's back. The donkey didn't move.

"Get him up! Get him up!" the boys chanted.

The miner fumbled for something in his pocket. The donkey pricked up its long ears. "Hee-haw! Hee-haw!" it screamed.

Suddenly the donkey jumped up, sending its master sprawling backward. The miner got up unhurriedly. When he again reached into his pocket, the donkey came around and eagerly licked its master's hand.

"Hurrah!" The boys shouted, flinging their hats into the air.

The miner adjusted a worn blanket around the donkey's belly. He collected his belongings and strapped the hardware to the donkey's back. Without a single profanity, he rubbed dirt from the seat of his pants and mounted the donkey.

The boys clapped. "He did it! He did it!"

When the miner got the donkey moving, he lifted his crumpled hat to the carriage. Vienna gasped. It *was* Zeke! Turning the donkey around, Zeke rode alongside

Mrs. Graham. "Ma'am, you remind me of my angel mother. It does a feller good to see a fine woman like that." He had to shout over the din caused by his rattling household goods.

"Your angel mother? Did she die?" Mrs. Graham also raised her voice to be heard.

"Gone and died, ma'am. I shoulda stayed home instead of grubbin' for gold. I shoulda taken care of my ma."

"Don't blame yourself, young man. You didn't know—"

"Mighty obliged for them good words, ma'am." Zeke lifted his hat to Mrs. Graham and clattered off in the opposite direction.

Vienna couldn't miss Zeke's crestfallen expression on seeing her beside Phil. She shivered. If John saw her beside Phil, might he not also jump to the wrong conclusion?

Priscilla giggled in the back seat. "Who was that, Mother?"

"He didn't say, but he made an impression we shan't easily forget." Mrs. Graham sounded amused.

Vienna glanced over her shoulder. "I know him, Mrs. Wilson—uh, I mean Mrs. Graham. He's a gold miner who struck it rich. His name is Zeke."

"Zeke." Mrs. Graham let the name roll off her tongue.

"How rich is he?" Priscilla wanted to know.

"My brother Elisha says he must be very rich indeed. That boy is rarely wrong. He's smart." Vienna spoke with pride.

"Is he one of the twins?" Mrs. Graham asked.

"He is."

"Is Zeke moving to this area?" Priscilla wanted to know.

Vienna shrugged. "I don't know."

"He was interesting," Priscilla admitted. Turning to her mother, she said, "I'd like to meet Zeke. Can you arrange it, Mother?"

Mrs. Graham sighed. "Sometimes you ask too much, Prissy."

Chapter Ten
Farmer's Son

Vienna tried hard to concentrate on her studies. Cold November wind blew through the window Molly had opened. Sitting at the desk, she tried to keep her papers from flying away. Priscilla paraded up and down the narrow room, balancing a book on her head and frequently bumping into Vienna's chair.

"Elbow to elbow," Priscilla complained. "This dormitory room is too small for three people."

"Why do you carry that silly book around? It makes you look ridiculous." Molly sat on the edge of her bed, boots dangling.

"Why do you insist on freezing us out?" Priscilla slammed the window shut, mumbling something about "fresh air fiend."

"Why do you carry that book around?" Molly asked again.

"I want good posture. I'm not a slouch like somebody else I know. That's why!"

"Posture!" Molly scoffed.

"It would do you no harm to become cilvilized," Priscilla needled her. "I've been watching you in the dining hall. You eat like a slob."

"I do not! I'm learning how to eat with a knife and fork, just like the rest of you."

Priscilla continued her parade. "I wish you were more mannerly. You're a disgrace to this school and to your family. What will you do when guests arrive and you must play the hostess?"

"I'll invite my big brothers," Molly countered. "My brothers don't care how I eat or walk. They grew up on the farm, and they'll be farmers on the land Pa is buying for them. They'll be my guests, if you must know."

Priscilla harrumphed. "What will you do when your stepmother comes for a visit?"

"She can be as proper as she likes," Molly sassed. "She better not tell me which knife or fork to use once I'm married and have my own home."

"I don't understand why you hate your stepmother." Priscilla was not going to quit. "I love my stepfather. Daddy's the greatest thing that ever happened to me. He doesn't even scold when I fuss with my hair."

"She told me I had to attend this academy," Molly pouted. "She said I'm an embarrassment."

"My stepfather is wonderful," Priscilla raved on. "Mother and I never had it so good."

"She wants Pa all to herself. I'm in her way," Molly grumbled, not even listening to Priscilla.

"Maybe she'd like you better if you weren't so . . ." Priscilla paused, her upturned little nose wrinkled.

"She hates me, and I hate her. It's the way I like it." Molly jumped down and fetched the guitar she kept on the empty upper bed.

"Some family!" Priscilla removed the book from her head and tossed it on her bed. "Maybe you hate your stepmother because she's taken your ma's place. Maybe you're grieving over your ma, just like Phil is grieving over our pa."

Molly burst into tears. "We had to leave Ma at the wayside," she sobbed. "We had to move on. My oldest brother stayed with Ma until she died."

"What did she die of?" Priscilla sounded subdued.

"Cholera."

"Terrible!" Priscilla shook her red mane. "Our pa got killed on the trail, but he had it coming. Picking a fight with another hothead was stupid. Why Phil is so broken up over Pa I'll never know. Pa used to beat Phil."

"I wouldn't care if my ma beat me," Molly wailed. "Now that she's gone, she can't even do that." Molly strummed her guitar. "If it wasn't for this guitar I'd go crazy."

Vienna put her papers aside. "I hope the two of you are through bickering. All of us grew up on a farm, and now we want to learn something new. Let's make good use of our time. Let's study! That's what we came here for."

Priscilla gathered her sheet music. "Quit torturing that poor guitar, Molly. You sound awful."

"I do not!" Molly defended herself. "The music teacher says I'm making progress."

"The music teacher is a bore. She's never satisfied with my playing." Priscilla whirled out the door and danced down the stairs.

Molly let out her breath. "Thank goodness, she's off. She gets to me—too much talk, too much useless energy."

"Priscilla is lively, all right, but she's a nice girl, Molly," Vienna defended her friend. "You mustn't mind her quirks. She doesn't mean what she says."

"She's always picking on me," Molly complained.

"She can be a good friend, Molly. I've known her since grade school. I know."

Molly frowned. "Why doesn't she let on that she's my friend?"

"Perhaps she'll let you ride in the carriage some time. Would you like that, Molly?"

"Get out of this jail? You bet I'd like that!" Molly put the guitar on the empty bed and reopened the window. "Ah, I love good air!"

Vienna gave herself a push. "I've been wanting to talk to you, Molly."

"To me? What about?" Molly's eyebrows shot up.

"Do you, uh, remember passing through the Rockies when wagon trains banded together for safety?"

"Yes. Why do you ask?"

"Do you remember a blond guide by the name of John Zumwalt? He rode beside your wagon, and you sat by his campfire."

"John? Did he have a younger brother?"

"And a mother."

"How do you know about John? Were you in the same train?"

"I followed in a wagon behind you, Molly. You laughed so heartily that everybody heard you."

Molly looked puzzled. "What is your interest in John?"

"We, uh, got engaged at the place where emigrant trains from St. Louis joined our party."

Molly shrugged. "That was long before I met John."

Vienna's heart hammered. "Do you know where John is, Molly? Would you tell me if you knew?"

"I haven't the faintest idea what happened to John. Our wagons separated at Sutter's Fort in the valley of the Sacramento." Molly scrutinized Vienna. "Were you jealous of me?"

"No, of course not." Vienna swallowed. She hated to broach the next touchy subject, but it had to be done. "I've been wanting to ask you. What happened the day you carried a food tray to John's wagon? What was his mother like?"

Molly turned deep red. "That one! She's a monster, I tell you. Live with a woman like that under one roof? Not me!"

Vienna felt a kick in her stomach. John did everything for his mother, the widow who suffered from sick headaches. If she, Vienna, ever met John's dear old mother, how could she win her over?

On an overcast November day Phil and Mrs. Graham drove up the graveled drive in front of the school. The governess escorted Priscilla and Vienna outside.

Priscilla took the back seat beside her mother. "Oh, Mother, I'm so glad you came!"

"Your daddy asked me to attend to some business, darling. He wasn't able to come, but he sends his love." Mrs. Graham's forearms folded in a comfortable gesture, one wrist resting easily on the other, showing smooth, veined hands. She lifted her chin, smiling graciously. "Why don't you join my son, Vienna?"

"Thank you, Mrs. Graham," Vienna said and climbed up.

Every trip gave her opportunity to look for John. While Mrs. Graham and Priscilla made small talk and Phil kept up his sullen silence, she sleuthed for clues that could lead her to her golden hero.

"Whoa!" Phil called to the horses, stopping at the local branch of the Grahams' bank.

Mrs. Graham gathered her skirts and alighted. "Wait for me, Phil. I may be a while."

"Yes, Ma."

"'Mother,'" she corrected him.

Phil scowled. "I'll wait, Ma."

Priscilla dashed after her mother, and Vienna rose to get a better view.

"What are you looking for?" Phil asked.

Vienna paused, unable to believe Phil had spoken to her.

"I asked what you're looking for," he repeated.

"Nothing." Vienna felt rattled.

Phil grasped her sleeve and pulled her down beside him. "I have something to tell you."

Vienna extricated herself from his grip. "You never spoke to me before."

"It's 'cause I've been thinking."

"About what?"

"You and me. We've grown up on a farm. We've known each other a long time."

"So we have, Phil." What was he getting at? The strange look in his eyes rang a warning bell.

"How do you feel about me, Vienna?"

"You mean, do I like you? Of course I like you. You're my best friend's brother."

"I've known you since you were a kid," Phil reminded her. "You used to drop in and play with Priss."

"We also met at the Sabbath service," she added.

"You were a nice little girl, Vienna. You always gave in when Priss acted up. You were the peacemaker."

"You remember all that?"

"That and more," Phil nodded. "Priss never quit talking about you. She'd say, 'Vienna has all the luck. She's meeting young gentlemen on her journey.'"

Vienna felt warm. She had met one gentleman who counted. Despite the hardships, she had been lucky.

"If it wasn't for you, we'd still be in Michigan," Phil mused, looking sullen again. "If it wasn't for you, Pa would still be alive."

"I'm sorry about your pa, Phil, but his death is not my fault."

Phil backed down. "All right. I can't get used to life in this big-city hellhole, Vienna. More saloons than churches. Dishonest men, profiteers, murderers—that's not for me."

"I understand, Phil. You went through a lot, and you feel bitter. I wouldn't want to live in San Francisco myself."

"I want a farm," Phil stated, "a spread like Pa had, where a man can raise good kids and build his house with the help of neighbors."

Vienna nodded.

He paused. "I used to admire your ma. Now there was a woman who worked alongside her man and brought up her children right."

"Thank you, Phil." Vienna felt warm inside.

"Your ma is a pretty woman, tall and slim. She is like you, Vienna, a woman a man can be proud of."

Vienna avoided Phil's direct look. "Father is proud of her."

"You're like your ma, Vienna." Phil's violet eyes flashed. Two white teeth showed through his carefully groomed and waxed mustache.

Vienna fidgeted. She didn't know how to interpret Phil's half smile. "What are you getting at?" she asked finally.

"Mr. Graham wants me to become a banker. I'm not cut out for that, Vienna. I'm a farmer in city clothes."

"You are a flashy dresser all right." Vienna edged away.

"I look like Ma wants me to. When I get my farm I'll wear overalls and shave off this silly mustache. I hate looking like a dude." He shrugged, looking glum. "Clothes only go so far, Vienna. What I need is a wife, a farm, and children."

"Why are you telling me all this, Phil?"

"It's 'cause there are things I like about you, Vienna. You don't talk too much. I can't stand women who jabber all the time. You don't flutter around like Priss. She drives me crazy." He drew in a breath, then added, "You don't make up to boys, and you don't gussy yourself up like Priss. I can't stand it when women play the fashion queen."

"What's the point of all this, Phil? First, you don't talk to me, and now you are the fluent speaker." Vienna eyed him carefully. "Why did you give me all those sidelong glances without ever saying a word?"

"Don't blame me, Vienna. I can't look at you enough 'cause you're so proud and pretty. I keep thinking, *What's she going to say when I ask her?*" He pulled up his shoulders in an uncomfortable gesture. "I don't know how to ask you."

"Ask me what?" Vienna wished Mrs. Graham would come back.

"That I want you for my wife."

Vienna gulped.

"I could make it with a girl like you," Phil said earnestly. "You're strong, like your ma. You'll have sons. Marry me, Vienna! You won't regret it. We'll build a house and plant fruit trees, and maybe even a palm tree or two. The loam is deep in the valley south of the Bay. Anything will grow in that warm climate."

"But I—" Vienna stammered.

His face fell. "Are you spoken for?"

Vienna nodded. "His name is John, and I'll marry him."

Chapter Eleven
A Letter From Home

Muddy roads kept Mrs. Graham from visiting during the spring rains of 1856. Vienna was glad. She dreaded seeing Phil, fearing she had hurt his feelings. She pleaded with Priscilla to let Molly come along the next time they had an outing.

"The girl has had tough going," she told Priscilla. "Imagine, losing your mother."

Priscilla frowned. "I cannot imagine losing my mother."

"My young brothers and I would have perished without our mother," Vienna continued. "You can't imagine the problems we ran into on our way to California. With the Lord's help, Mother weathered them all."

Priscilla wrapped coppery strands around her moistened finger, creating stunning curls. "I do feel sorry for Molly," she admitted. "It's just that she's so crude. I hate to be seen in her company."

"If you show Molly that you're her friend she'll feel better, Priss. We may not see her again after graduation. You know how she hates this place. Let's give her a good memory."

Priscilla let out a sigh. "I'll tell Mother that Molly's father is doing business with Daddy."

"That's my Priss." Vienna hugged her friend. Whenever Priscilla smiled her pixie smile, Vienna forgot to be angry.

Priscilla giggled. "The drive will be educational, don't you think?" She hunted for her sheet music in a cluttered corner. "I've gotta run, or I'll be late."

Her footsteps quickly faded away down the hall, replaced by measured steps approaching the door. The governess knocked.

"A letter for Miss Brooks," she announced.

Vienna tingled. News from home! She hadn't heard from her family during the long, soggy winter. She tore the letter open.

Dear daughter Vienna,

We hope you are doing well at the academy. You will love to know that you have a new baby brother. We named him Joseph, Joey for short. The twins built a cottage for us near the garden. Your father and I feel like loafers without our cows. Elisha and Elijah are working at a mountain sawmill.

Vienna put the letter down. Tears stung her eyes. Elisha and Elijah laboring at a mountain sawmill? She couldn't bear the thought. Elisha, that upright boy, stagnating in crude company? She had hoped he might find a position as a clerk, or even fulfill Mother's fondest dream. Why couldn't Elisha become a teacher? Why couldn't he attend academy? She put her head on her arms and sobbed. Drying her tears, she read on.

Can you find a job to tide you over until fall, daughter? Your tuition is paid for the second year; however, there isn't any travel money just now. See what you can do.

Your loving mother

There was a postscript: *Our sweet peas are blooming, and the rosebushes are covered in buds.*

It was like Mother to add a cheerful note. Vienna ached for Mother's closeness. A hug, a smile, the little gifts

Mother gave her for no special reason at all had always given her such happiness.

Why were there no cows? Why had the family moved? Why were the twins working at the sawmill? If the cows had been sold, why was there no money? Mother didn't say.

She yearned for a word from her brothers and fretted about the boys' future. She couldn't imagine Elisha in the company of coarse and godless men. And what about Elmont, the youngster, who expressed terror at the sight of men? What would become of that precious boy?

She felt ashamed for having accepted her brothers' tuition money. The boys themselves should be studying. She could always get married.

Cold shivers trickled down Vienna's spine. Perhaps she should have encouraged Jeffrey. Their former teamster had offered to help her family with money. Perhaps she should marry Zeke, who had money and a good heart to boot. Perhaps she should consider Phil, on whose future place her family might be welcome. Phil admired Mother.

Mother's words "Always listen to your own conscience" came to Vienna's rescue. And her conscience was shouting, "I love John and want to marry him!"

Bowing her head, she prayed, "Dear God, please let Elisha fulfill my mother's dream. Let him become a teacher. Please, take care of all my brothers."

Mother's letter was shielding Vienna from disastrous news. The unthinkable had happened: miners lost faith in Bidwell Bar's gold deposits. Some 3,000 miners and townfolk stampeded to Ophir, soon renamed Oroville, "City of Gold." The county seat was moved from Bidwell Bar to Oroville, and the former boomtown became a ghost town. In desperate efforts to save the family business, the twins delivered milk to Oroville, weathering a 10-mile ride twice a day on their ponies, in addition to doing the herding.

One day during a howling spring storm the cows and ponies were taken from the Brookses and the bankrupted family was forced to move out. Father hobbling on crutches, Mother carrying the new baby, and the boys shivering in wet clothes, left their home in the lashing rain. Destitute, with bundles on their backs, they trudged up the path to the garden.

Mother wrapped the squalling baby in her shawl and sought refuge in the three-foot-square toolshed the twins had built. The boys gathered slabs of bark to cover themselves for the night. The next morning the family breakfasted on vegetables pulled from the garden, then moved to a nearby spring, where the twins had stored scrap lumber for a shelter they planned to build.

Elisha and Elijah spent five days building a cottage to shelter the family. After the first night, Father sent the twins to the mountain sawmill. "People must eat and boys must work," he said.

Vienna heaved a sigh. She stepped to the window. The botany class was getting ready to plant a hedge around the fence. Under the botany teacher's supervision, the students spaded the ground and proceeded to put in young shrubs.

A big girl arrived late. She was carrying a scythe over her shoulder and a whetstone in the leather belt around her waist. The teacher pointed to weeds and grasses that had sprung up during the rains.

Vienna recognized Molly. The girl expertly swung the scythe, seeming to enjoy the smell of the freshly cut grass. Red-cheeked, she stopped every so often to sharpen the blade. Vienna perched on the windowsill. Listening to the lusty swishing sounds made by Molly's scythe, she wondered how she could pay for ferry service and stagecoach. She couldn't bear the idea of not seeing her family for another year.

In the midst of examinations, she felt like running away. Helping Mother with the new baby seemed more important than studying at an academy. She had promised Father she'd come home for summer vacation. But how could she travel without money? She thought of Jeffrey's buggy and Phil's carriage. Fretting about her family and despairing over her fruitless search for John, she felt this sudden driving need for action.

On graduation day many girls packed up and left right after the ceremonies. Vienna fervently wished she could head home too. She and her roommates had arranged to stay another day.

"How are we going to spend the day?" Vienna asked without enthusiasm.

"Let's have English High Tea on the porch," Molly suggested. "I'll play my guitar."

"Oh, no! I've heard enough of your guitar playing. Let's think of something better," Priscilla pleaded.

The debate was ended when the governess announced the arrival of Mrs. Graham. Vienna noticed Molly's stricken look.

"Can Molly come along for the ride, Priss?"

"Don't be silly," Priscilla said, wrinkling her nose.

"Please, take me along, Priscilla! I haven't been outside since they dragged me in here, and tomorrow I'll be stuck with my stepmother." Molly was actually begging.

"Well, all right. Why not give Mother and Phil a good laugh?"

"'Bye," said Vienna. "Have a good time."

Priscilla raised her brows. "There's room for you in the carriage."

Once outside, Vienna nudged Molly onto the driver's seat. Phil flipped the reins, and the carriage clattered over the curved drive toward the street.

Excitedly, Molly pointed this way and that way. "Look at this, Phil! Look at that, Phil!" she cried. When he continued to look straight ahead in his sullen way, she grabbed his arm and made him pay attention. "Say something, you stupid lug!"

Phil pulled away in apparent disgust.

Molly thrust her elbow into his side. "Well, do you like it? Answer me! I asked you something."

Phil flinched. "I like it," he grunted.

Priscilla whispered into Vienna's ear, "Molly treats Phil like one of her own brothers. She's so uncouth."

Again, Molly pointed. "Hey, did you see that, Phil? Did you see it?"

Phil grunted an answer, prompting Molly to sound her loud, cackling laugh.

Phil stopped the horses. "Hold the reins," he told Molly and jumped from the carriage and walked toward a store.

"I'm out of mustache wax," he said in answer to his mother's questioning look.

Minutes went by while they waited for Phil.

Suddenly Molly grabbed the reins and yelled "Giddyup!"

"What are you doing?" Priscilla screeched. "Wait for Phil!"

Molly glanced over her shoulder, hazel eyes agleam. Phil was running after the carriage, holding on to his hat and waving a small package.

Molly stopped the horses. "Next time you hurry up," she commanded. "I'm not used to boys who linger at the store."

"Poor Phil; she's not his type." Priscilla's green eyes shot darts.

Catching Mrs. Graham's astonished look, Vienna felt an apology was needed. "I'm sorry I talked Priss into bringing her along, Mrs. Graham," she said.

A buggy drew up beside them. Instead of overtaking the carriage, the driver called out. "A very good afternoon to you, ma'am. I've been trying to settle an account, being that my conscience bothers me."

"Jeffrey? Is that you?" Mrs. Graham clicked her Chinese sun umbrella shut.

"Yes, ma'am. Please accept the long overdue repayment of your generous loan." Jeffrey flung a drawstring purse into Mrs. Graham's lap.

Mrs. Graham opened the bag. Gold coins glinted in the sun. "Why, Jeffrey, this is more than I gave you."

"Capital and interest, ma'am." He looked past Mrs. Graham. "Vienna Brooks, how extraordinary to see you here!" He discreetly appraised Priscilla.

"My daughter," Mrs. Graham introduced. "You remember Priscilla, don't you, Jeffrey?"

"A surprise, ma'am. She has turned into an exquisite beauty. She takes after you, ma'am."

Mrs. Graham smiled.

Jeffrey pulled ahead to make room for an oncoming wagon and disappeared in the traffic.

Priscilla craned her neck. "Why is he dressed like that, Mother? He looks elegant and prosperous. Why, he was in rags when we last saw him."

"Jeffrey is no longer broke, darling," Mrs. Graham laughed. "Your daddy told me about Jeffrey. The young man bought out his partners and already owns three saloons at the waterfront."

"Is there money in saloons, Mother?"

"There certainly is, darling. Foolish men waste their earnings in drinking and gambling saloons. Jeffrey will be rich in no time, ambitious as he is."

"Jeffrey rich?" Priscilla faced Vienna. "Did you expect that from your former teamster?"

"No, I didn't. Jeffrey was so poor he didn't even own a horse." Vienna smiled. "The other men called him 'Milk Face.'"

Mrs. Graham snapped open her umbrella. "Ambitious men with the right connections can make their fortunes in California." She lowered her voice. "Mr. Steele, for example, arrived penniless. Now he's an importer."

"Molly says he's rich," Priscilla whispered back. "Is that so, Mother?"

Mrs. Graham smiled comfortably. "Rich enough to marry an educated lady from the States and send his daughter to an academy and college should she desire further education."

Priscilla snickered. "Molly?"

Mrs. Graham made an ample gesture. "You never know, darling. People can change."

"I want to meet Jeffrey again," Priscilla decided. "Can you arrange it, Mother?"

"I'll try, darling."

Why did Priscilla want to grab a rich man? Vienna wondered. Why was Priscilla so fascinated with everything rich? She decided to include her friend in her prayers. She thought that perhaps God used Priscilla to test her patience.

Molly and Priscilla departed the following morning. "See you in the fall," they told Vienna, rushing off to their parents' carriages.

Vienna had obtained permission to leave without a parent or guardian claiming her. She half expected to see Zeke at the entrance. "He's probably trying his luck on some new claim," she muttered.

She found work in a dry-goods store. She wanted to learn about selling, customer relations, and running a store. Before long, the proprietor commented that more men and women than ever dropped in to shop. "You're good for my business," he praised her.

One foggy summer morning Jeffrey stopped his buggy outside. Had she changed her mind? he asked. Could he come again and see her? Upon hearing Vienna's firm no, he drove off as if chased by the devil.

"That little feller is hot under the collar," Vienna's employer observed. "He's got a chip on his shoulder, wants to be bigger than his breeches."

"How can you tell?" Vienna asked.

"Didn't you see his high-heeled boots under the city clothes?" The man chuckled. "That fellow will never grow up to your height, Vienna."

The day Phil and Zeke stopped in together the proprietor

appeared delighted. "Sell them all you can," he encouraged.

Vienna showed Zeke shirts and overalls. She showed Phil bolts of cloth.

While Zeke tried on his overalls in the back room, Phil addressed Vienna. "Have you changed your mind? I am offering you a farm and security, and I'm not expecting any dowry."

"I told you before, Phil, I am engaged to John, and I am true to him." Vienna sounded firm.

"What about that gold miner?" Phil stabbed his thumb toward the back room.

"Zeke?"

"Whatever. What did you tell him?"

"'No.'"

Phil sullenly fingered the flowered muslin he had been considering. "I don't want it," he said. Pouting, he left the store and paced the wooden sidewalk out front.

Zeke emerged from the back room, overalls slung over his shoulder. "They fit fine, Miss Vienna. I'll take them."

Vienna quoted the price, took his money, and returned the change. Zeke pointed to the window. His donkey stood at the hitching post, long ears flopping at Phil, who was pacing up and down the raised wooden sidewalk.

"What about him? Who's he?" Zeke pointed at Phil. "I saw you beside him on that carriage."

"Phil is my girlfriend's brother," Vienna replied. "I've known him since childhood. There's nothing between us."

"What about John? Has he come around yet?" Zeke clamped the overalls under his arm.

Vienna swallowed. "I, uh, haven't seen him yet."

"It's been four years," Zeke pointed out. "Ain't no man gonna wait four years for a woman."

"You have been waiting for me almost a year," Vienna told him.

"That's different. You're flesh and blood. He's a ghost you're droolin' over."

"John is no ghost, and I am not drooling!" Vienna retorted.

"No offense, Miss Vienna." Zeke's eyes took in the store. "I hate for you to slave in this place. I kin give you a better life." He pinched his crumpled hat.

"Is there anything else, Zeke?"

"I'm powerful lonesome, Miss Vienna. If I had a wife to take care of I'd be a tremendous feller." He scuffed his boots. "You're the girl I've been hankering after. Say we'll be joined in the holy bonds and forget John. I kin protect you."

"You're a good person, Zeke. I appreciate all you're trying to do, but I am engaged."

"Let me know if you change your mind. I'll be stoppin' by." Zeke's boots dragged on the plank floor on his way to the exit.

Feeling sorry for the miner, Vienna meant to call after him, but Zeke headed straight for Phil. The two chatted for some time before heading for donkey and carriage. What were they discussing? Vienna wondered.

Chapter Twelve
Secrets

Vienna's employer tossed her bag onto his wagon. "You really want to go back to school?" he asked. "You could be working and making money instead."

Vienna sensed his reluctance to let her go. "I must complete academy and get my degree," she insisted. "My family would never forgive me if I took the easy way out."

"Have it your way."

He drove her to the academy and parked his wagon at the street side. Buggies and carriages were unloading students and luggage on the curved drive leading up to the academy's entrance. Drivers kept horses in check as parents bade daughters goodbye.

Vienna's employer carried her bag to the entrance. "Come back after you graduate, you hear? Consider yourself rehired."

"If I'm not getting married first," Vienna laughed.

They shook hands, and she thanked him for his kindness.

Glad to be back, Vienna looked around. The bushes and saplings planted by last year's botany class softened the facade of the two-story structure. The bright September sun reflected from the gable end with its board-and-batten walls, casting shadows on the columned porch. Bags cluttered the porch while their owners stood in line for registration.

Vienna looked for Priscilla and Molly and felt hugely disappointed when she didn't see them. Weren't her friends attending this year?

The janitor carried Vienna's bag upstairs and set it inside her former room. Once again she picked up the scent of lavender—Priscilla stood at the window. Head turned to one side, she displayed her pixie smile.

"I've been waiting for you, Vienna. Look what I got!" Priscilla held a frilly cuff to Vienna's face. "Look! Isn't it absolutely beautiful?"

A golden filigree ring shimmered on Priscilla's tiny ring finger.

"Did your mother give it to you?" Vienna asked.

Priscilla shook her red curls. "No, silly!"

"Your stepfather?"

"Of course not!" Priscilla grew impatient. "It's from Jeffrey. We're engaged!"

"You and Jeffrey?"

"And what's wrong with that?" Priscilla's face reddened. "Just because you knew him first doesn't mean you own him."

"Don't get mad, Priss. I meant no harm. Congratulations! The ring is beautiful."

The girls embraced.

"I'm so happy, Vienna. I couldn't wait to tell you. This is going to be a fun year."

Priscilla's happy mood changed abruptly as coughing and wheezing sounds grew loud at the door and Fran entered. The year before, in spite of her pleading, Priscilla had made her move out because Fran's coughing and wheezing got on her nerves.

"What are you doing here?" Priscilla demanded.

Fran held up the information sheet students received

at the registration desk. Her name was listed beside the room number.

"Don't unpack," Priscilla huffed. "I'll straighten out this mess."

She dashed off and returned with the janitor, who whisked Fran's bag out of the room and beckoned the girl to follow him down the hall.

"How did you manage that, Priss?" Vienna frowned. She felt sorry for Fran.

"Daddy gives money to this school; they better listen to me." Priscilla's nose wrinkled. "Time to unpack, I suppose."

"Who else will share our room?" Vienna hesitated before putting her belongings into the chest of drawers.

"I have no idea, but I know that I hate having to put up with strangers."

"What about Molly? Isn't she coming?"

Priscilla studied the information sheet. "They put Molly into another room. I'll fix that!" She dashed off once more, returning with a young lady.

Vienna's mouth fell open. "Is that you, Molly?"

"In the flesh." Molly pivoted happily. The girl's hair was brushed off her neck and gathered into a stylish knot. A lace choker hugged her throat like strings of delicate white pearls. Her flat and angular features were cleverly disguised by the rounded shapes of her dress.

"How did you do it?" Vienna exclaimed.

"My stepmother gave me tips on how to style my hair, and she took me to her own seamstress." Molly laughed a remarkably subdued laugh. "Even the governess didn't recognize me," she chortled.

Priscilla's eyebrows arched. "Your stepmother?"

Molly blushed. "She's really quite nice—almost like an older sister. We have things in common now."

"Well, what do you know!" Priscilla breathed.

The janitor brought Molly's bags. Arranging dainty things in the drawer she shared with Vienna, Molly held an aromatic sachet to Vienna's nose. "Smell!"

"Mmmm!" Vienna recalled fragrances from her mother's garden. "I love it, Molly."

"My stepmother gave it to me," Molly boasted.

Priscilla looked unhappy. "I guess from now on you'll play the spoiled rich girl," she muttered.

When Molly ignored the remark, Priscilla triumphantly showed her the ring. "I am engaged," she announced.

Molly stared. "To whom?"

"Jeffrey, of course."

"Vienna's former teamster?"

"Who is now the wealthy proprietor of prospering businesses," Priscilla corrected. "Jeff says he'll build me a mansion because I'm the prettiest girl around," Priscilla beamed. "Jeff is fun. He tells terrific tales of his seafaring adventures and—"

"Did he tell you what happened at Kanesville on the Missouri?" Vienna interrupted.

Priscilla scowled. "I don't blame Jeff a bit for turning back to the States. He used his head. Why, he could have gotten himself killed in Indian country."

"You made it through Indian country, Priss."

Priscilla's eyes narrowed. "Pa didn't make it, and neither did Molly's ma."

"Sorry, Priss. I just want you to know what you may be getting yourself into with Jeffrey. You hardly know him."

"If I didn't know you better, I'd say you're jealous, Vienna. Jeff has his strengths. You don't know the wonderful qualities he has."

"Such as?"

"Jeff can take a setback and joke about it," Priscilla began. "He is tenacious and doesn't give up easily. He makes the best of a bad situation, and he's alert to opportunity. Daddy says Jeffrey knows how to handle people. Jeff gets what he wants."

"When did he develop all these qualities?" Vienna asked.

"In his childhood, of course."

"He never mentioned his childhood."

"It's because he's embarrassed about it. Jeff was a foundling. In the family that raised him he had to compete with the other kids. He learned early on how to make up to people just to survive." Priscilla smiled. "All along, Jeff dreamed of becoming rich some day so he wouldn't have to grovel anymore and people wouldn't care whether or not his parents deserted him."

Vienna wondered if Priscilla knew about the day Jeffrey had dropped in at the store. Determined to keep silent about Jeffrey's visit she asked, "Did Jeffrey come to court you?"

"Jeff has dealings with Daddy," Priscilla explained. "Mother invited him for lunch, and he drove me around in his buggy. It was fun."

Priscilla stepped close to Vienna. "Get yourself a rich husband, Vienna. You'll have an easy life and people will respect you."

Vienna backed up. "People respect my mother, Eliza Ann Scholfield Brooks," she said firmly. "I am just like my mother, Priss. I'll marry the man I truly love and will stand by him. I don't need a mansion. All I need is a loving husband and God-fearing children."

Priscilla's freckles blurred into angry red blotches. "Are you telling me that your mother is better than mine?" she challenged.

"Oh, Priss! Your mother is a fine lady. I like and respect her a lot. Why, it must have been terrible for her to see your pa dying with a gunshot wound. I think she's coping admirably. After all, she gave you and Phil a home."

Priscilla calmed down. "How did we get on this subject?"

"You told me to get a rich husband."

"What's so terrible about that?"

"You know that I'm waiting for John." Vienna paused. "Why is being rich so important to you?"

"Who am I, Vienna, actually?" Priscilla pulled off her

shoes and reached for her slippers. "I'm a backwoods girl city folk would laugh at if they knew. Who'd be impressed if I told them that I milked cows, washed milk buckets, and cleaned the barn? Who'd love and respect me?"

"I love you and I respect you," Vienna said quietly.

Priscilla threw herself into Vienna's arms. Blinking back tears, she said, "That's different, of course. You're from the backwoods yourself."

"Oh, Priss, cheer up!"

"That's easy for you to say. Jeff said I was *horrid* back in Michigan."

"You weren't horrid, Priss. You just had a temper sometimes." Vienna felt sorry for her friend. The girl was all right underneath her frilly varnish, she knew. "You're pretty and you're good," Vienna stressed. "You don't have to put on airs. People like you the way you are."

"You really think so?" Priscilla's lips stopped trembling.

"I know so." Vienna felt relief at seeing her friend's pixie smile.

September's warm days and cold nights passed quickly. Before October rains settled the dust, Mrs. Graham called at the academy and invited the girls for a ride.

Molly ran down the hall ahead of her roommates. On the staircase, she lifted her skirts and took two steps at a time. She slowed down on the porch, though, and approached the carriage with composure.

"Thank you for inviting me, Mrs. Graham; it was very gracious of you, ma'am," she said demurely.

"Molly Steele?" Mrs. Graham looked the girl over, smiling broadly. Her small teeth, filed down by some San Francisco dentist, sparkled in her mouth. "You're welcome to sit beside my son, dear. Why don't you climb up!"

Molly curtsied and climbed up with decorum. Phil gave her a dazed look as she sat down meekly beside him.

Priscilla's mother was on her way to a branch of the Grahams' bank in the nearby city of Oakland. Vienna welcomed the new route. Perhaps this time she'd find her golden hero!

They drove by a construction area. Hammers clicked and saws grated. Mules, carts, and wagons moved about in clouds of dust. Foremen shouted orders. Carpenters putting up sidewalks before the winter rains carried on a cheerful banter. Horseback riders jingled their spurs, and express messengers hurried by with packages.

What a place! Vienna tingled with excitement as she tried to take it all in. Businesses lined the street—mercantile establishments and blacksmith shops, with horses and mules standing at hitching posts. Women and children walked to and fro.

Then a cry escaped Vienna's lips. On a board hammered across a storefront she saw the greatest marvel of all: a sign advertising the BIG Z.

Was John in this nearby city? Could it be?

"Let me off, Phil!" she cried. "Stop!"

"Whoa!" Phil called to the horses as Vienna nearly tumbled from the carriage.

Priscilla ran after her and grabbed her arm. "Where are you going?"

"Over there! That's John's store!"

The girls dashed up the raised wooden sidewalk and into the store. An older woman stood behind the counter.

"May I help you?" she asked.

"Are you Mrs. Zumwalt? Are you John's mother?" Vienna asked timidly.

"Yes, I am."

Priscilla giggled. "My friend is sweet on John. She came to see him. Is he around?"

Mrs. Zumwalt gave Vienna a withering look. "John has proposed to a girl who will be his wife," she said firmly. "He has no use for a silly young thing that comes around to flirt."

Vienna felt sick to her stomach. John engaged? She had come too late!

Once outside, she turned on Priscilla. "Why do you act so crazy at times? Why did you say such a stupid thing?"

"A good thing I did! Now you know where you stand." Priscilla ran across the street, dodging horses and wagons.

Mrs. Graham folded the umbrella that had shielded her fair face from the rays of the October sun. "Well?"

"The store belongs to the Zumwalts, Mother. Vienna found John!" Priscilla gushed.

Phil turned around as Vienna climbed into the carriage. "Why didn't you bring him out so we could meet him?"

"He wasn't in," Priscilla explained. "Only his mother was in the store."

"Was she nice?" Molly wanted to know.

"Nice?" Priscilla made a face.

"I told you so, Vienna! She's a mean old woman." Molly sounded satisfied.

Back at the academy, Vienna threw herself into her studies. In a quiet hour when Priscilla and Molly were off to their music lessons, she brooded about her future. Could she fulfill her mother's ambition? Could she become a teacher? Visions of spinsterhood and loneliness bothered Vienna. She couldn't imagine herself as a schoolmarm. On the verge of tears, she took out her diary and confided her unhappiness. What kind of husband would Zeke or Phil make, or even Jeffrey? She quickly erased the question from her mind. The loved one in whom she'd confide her troubles would have to be John. Steps creaked in the hall outside. Thinking her roommates were returning, Vienna slipped her diary under her pillow. When the steps passed her door, she peeked out. Fran was walking to her room, wheezing.

Seeing Fran's slumped shoulders, she sensed the girl's unhappiness. Without much forethought, Vienna walked to the end of the hall and knocked on Fran's door. "It's me—Vienna. Please let me in, Fran."

"C-come in!"

Vienna entered, bidding a cheerful hello.

Fran was perched on the windowsill, ready to embroider a throw pillow. Alarm jumped into the girl's eyes. "What do you want? Is your friend telling me to move out again?"

"No, Fran. I came for a friendly visit."

"Why?"

"I thought perhaps you needed a friend." Vienna looked about the spotless room. Not a thing out of place! Only a coverlet on a lower bed and a framed daguerreotype on the desk indicated that the room was lived in. "Do you live here all by yourself, Fran?"

"Nobody wants to move in with me, Vienna."

"I'm sorry, Fran." Vienna stepped to the window that looked out over the delivery entrance. A burly man was unloading goods from a wagon. "Let me see your embroidery," Vienna asked.

Fran held up a nearly completed throw pillow covered with tiny stitches.

"Home, Sweet Home," Vienna read. "Are you making the pillow for your mother?"

Fran started to cough.

"Did I say something wrong, Fran? Are you making the pillow for yourself? For your hope chest maybe?"

"My mother died of childbed fever after I was born," Fran said.

Vienna felt as though she had been struck by lightning. Collecting herself, she pointed to the daguerreotype. "Is this your stepmother?"

Fran shook her head. "Dad never remarried."

"Where does he live?"

"Nowhere. He's touring the gold country. He's an actor."

"Where do you live when you're not in school?"

"Dad always finds some family that takes me in, or some boardinghouse where I can stay."

Vienna's head whirred with questions. "Did you grow up in somebody else's family?"

"No, Dad kept me by his side. I had a nanny, but when we got off the ship in San Francisco she ran off with a miner. That's why Dad put me into this school." Fran's eyes reddened. "Nobody wants me. She didn't, and Dad doesn't either."

"How can you say that?"

"It's true. Dad blames me for my mother's death. If it hadn't been for me, she'd still be alive."

"Don't even think such a thing, Fran! Your mother's death wasn't your fault."

"He hates me anyway," Fran wheezed.

"What does he say, or do, to show it?"

"That's just it, Vienna. He lets on that he loves me. He's too good an actor to—"

"Hush!" Vienna gently set Fran's embroidery kit aside. She embraced the girl and rocked her as if she were a toddler. "Your dad loves you, Fran. He doesn't blame you at all. Why, if he didn't love you, he'd have put you on somebody else's doorstep. He'd have married again. Your dad made sacrifices because he truly loves you."

Fran's body untensed. "Why are you so good to me, Vienna? You're the only girl who's ever come into my room."

"I want to be your friend, Fran."

"What about the redhead? She'll hate you for speaking to me."

"Priscilla is all right, Fran. She has her quirks, but she'll outgrow them. I'm sorry you had to suffer because of her snap decisions. You'd have made a wonderful roommate for us."

Fran's face brightened. "You think so?"

On her way out, Vienna noticed that the girl wasn't wheezing or coughing anymore.

Chapter Thirteen
Revelations

Winter rains tapped at the dormitory window. Vienna sat at the edge of her bed studying and taking advantage of the candles flickering in Molly's candelabra. She wished she could use the desk, but Molly was writing a letter. Lately, Molly had spent hours at the desk, answering the mysterious letters she received.

Priscilla paraded up and down behind Molly, balancing a book on her head. At every turn she peeked over Molly's shoulder. "Whom are you writing to?" she pried.

Molly covered her stationery. "None of your business."

Priscilla tossed the book onto the bed. Her freckles blurred in her angry face. Priscilla's attitude toward Molly had changed. What was going on? Vienna wondered.

Then Priscilla leaned over Molly's shoulder and, lightning fast, she snatched up the letter Molly was writing.

"Give it back!" Molly screeched.

Priscilla held her off at arm's length.

"'Dear Phil,'" Priscilla read aloud. "'I can't wait until you start building our house in the South Bay. It will make a wonderful home for our children. I want to plant fruit trees and grapevines and lots of vegetables, and some berry bushes, if they will grow in that location. You can't imagine what it means to me, being able to live in the country again.'"

Priscilla's face grew dark. "They're planning to get married," she huffed. "Behind my back! Not even Mother knows about this. How do you like that, Vienna?"

Vienna offered no comment.

"Molly's wrong for Phil!" Priscilla ranted. "You'd think she's the boss the way she grabs his arm and makes him pay attention. Detestable! You, Vienna, would never do that. You're perfect for my brother, but no, he falls for that stupid Molly."

Molly pushed back her chair. "I'll have you know that Phil treats me with respect," she said hotly. "Phil loves me. Not only that, but he likes my pa, who's a farmer at heart. The two hit it off. I like farming, and I'm not afraid of work. I can give Phil the understanding he needs and the children he wants."

"Has he spoken to your pa already?" Priscilla's freckled cheeks grew fiery red, like her hair.

"Pa understands Phil, and so do I," Molly asserted. "Phil is a fish out of water in the city." Molly's eyes clouded. "Phil has been gulping for air in that hellhole called San Francisco. He's never been happy there."

"The city has a future," Priscilla countered. "It's a place where people can get rich. Someday you'll see great mansions up on those steep hills."

"Future or not, you can live in your mansion overlooking the waterfront. Phil and I want country air. Phil needs a place where honest men work up a sweat and neighbors get together in a friendly way."

"What do you know, Molly Steele waxes eloquent!" Priscilla's green eyes glittered.

Molly ignored the remark. "I'll have you know I'm exactly the right woman for Phil. I'm older than you girls, and Phil is older than your Jeffrey." Molly raised her hand, indicating she would allow no interruptions. "As for Vienna, she had her chance."

Priscilla whipped around. "Phil asked you?"

Vienna nodded. "I'm sorry, Priss, but Phil and I aren't right."

Priscilla hurled herself onto her bed, howling and pounding her pillow. "You're all against me," she sobbed. "I hate you, hate you, hate you!"

Vienna broke out in a sweat. She had lost John—while Molly and Priss had gained fiancés. And now Priscilla was carrying on.

"We cannot go on like this!" Vienna declared. "We're acting stupid when we could be best friends. Did either of you ever consider how my mother must feel, having left all the friends of her youth behind? Do we want to wind up like this—at each other's throats?"

Priscilla sat up and sniffled. "My mother doesn't have any childhood friends, either."

Molly looked dazed. "If Ma had survived, she wouldn't have any friends from back home."

Vienna brightened. "You see what I mean? We have a chance to be lifelong friends. Let's not ruin it. Go shake hands!"

Priscilla glowered at Molly. "You ask too much, Vienna," she huffed.

The next morning, neither Molly nor Priscilla was talking. Molly acted grumpy after getting up. Priscilla fussed with her hair, then gathered her sheet music and left minutes ahead of Molly.

"So much for friendship," Vienna muttered. She was contemplating a spectacular winter sunrise. The sky glowed in red hues as golden sunbursts triumphed over dark hills. She hoped for a sunny day until she remembered that red sunrises are followed by rain.

Sighing, she updated the diary she'd been neglecting lately. As she turned a page, the rosebud fell out. She picked it up without joy. What was the use of keeping the fragile thing? Even so, she reinserted the bud between the pages, knowing she'd never part with this reminder of her golden hero.

The sound of singing drifted up from the music room. The choir was practicing. Vienna had been given the hour off because her voice sounded raspy following a cold. She debated about what to write home.

Dear Mother,

I found and lost John all in the same day. You were right. He isn't coming for me. He's engaged to be married—to somebody else.

A great lump rose in her throat. Dare she state a fact so terrible it made her sick? She tore up the letter and started over.

Dear Mother,

Everything is fine here. I must be the poorest girl at the academy, but the teachers like me. I respect and obey them. I feel sure you'd agree with me when I say that they are fine educators. They truly care about the progress I am making. You are right: learning is important and teachers serve the common good. How are you getting along, Mother? Is Father well? I miss all of you. I would love to bounce my new baby brother. I wish I could collect wildflowers with my little brothers. Cheering you with flowers would give me great joy.

Vienna concluded the letter, lost in memories of her beloved family. Worries about Elisha crowded her mind. How could she get a message to him? If only the boy could read! Needing to get deep-down feelings off her chest, she picked up the diary and poured her heart out there.

Dear Brother Elisha,

Mother wants me to become a teacher. I have searched my innermost self and cannot see teaching in my future. If I find John, and he is agreeable, I will marry him, have his children, and work in his business. Perhaps you wonder why I am writing this letter to you. Well, of all my brothers, you are the most likely to fulfill our mother's dream. No, don't hastily say that this task cannot be accomplished. I have prayed about it and will continue to pray.

You may wonder why I direct my request to you and not to Elijah. For a good reason. Your twin brother is like you in many endearing ways, but there is a difference. While you both are generous and always ready to give something extra when you see a need, it is you God blessed with leadership ability. Your example has brought out the best in Elijah. You never shirk your duties when the going gets rough for you or for your charges.

More importantly, you know right from wrong. You never compromise when your conscience is at stake. As a teacher, you will imbue children with the values

Mother taught us. Children are growing up on a wild frontier. Mining camps are bad places for youngsters, as you well know. Unless they learn right from wrong, children will become godless adults, scoundrels who seek their own gain at the expense of others.

There is talk of schools opening up in many townships. Schools need dedicated teachers. Children need guidance. With your integrity and caring, you will make a fine educator, Elisha. You will never deny your beliefs. You will be the one to make our mother proud.

Please, Elisha, examine yourself. Pray about finding a way to become a credentialed teacher.

Your loving sister, Vienna.

She hesitated. Turning the page, she began another letter.

To the Angel of Elisha Brooks,

Please lead my brother to a fine school where he can obtain the education needed to qualify as a teacher. Please guide him in his future career. Prepare his way and protect him always.

Your grateful Vienna Brooks.

She felt better. The huge burden she had been carrying lifted from her shoulders.

The singing stopped in the music room below. Footsteps and voices grew loud in the hall. Vienna eased the diary under her pillow just as Priscilla burst into the room.

"Jeff ordered burned bricks from the States, Vienna! Imagine, his mansion will be fireproof and stand high on a hill. Jeff showed me the building site last summer. You should see the view! Fabulous!"

"I'm glad you're happy," Vienna said. Priscilla's pixie smile made her forget the girl's temper tantrums.

"Jeff and I will throw a big wedding and invite everybody when our mansion is finished. There'll be candles and fireplaces . . . More lights than you've ever seen!"

Vienna grinned. "I guess you'll have to write a thousand thank-you notes for your wedding gifts."

"I can't wait!" Priscilla dashed off, giggling.

Vienna added a postscript to her letter for Mother.

Priscilla says she will marry Jeffrey, our former teamster. He owns saloons and is making tons of money in the city.

Your loving daughter, Vienna.

She folded the paper, wrote the address in her best penmanship, then dribbled candle wax on the fold. She carried the letter to the reception desk and paid the required three cents for posting.

The rains stopped during the night. Vienna tossed. A donkey brayed out front. Zeke? Was he desperate to contact her? Zeke had visited her at the store repeatedly, always pressing for an answer.

Vienna slipped out of bed and reached for her moccasins. Careful not to wake her roommates, she tiptoed to the window. Clouds hurried across the sky, and a few stars sailed between them like little lost ships. The moon wasn't up yet. The braying stopped, and she forgot about Zeke. She waited for the moon.

Where was John this very minute? Was he perhaps whispering sweet nothings into his fiancée's ear? She went back to bed and cried herself to sleep.

Chapter Fourteen
Engagements

Spring 1857. Birds swooped in and out of nests underneath the eaves, feeding hungry fledglings. Vienna looked up from her studies. Unbidden thoughts disturbed her. The birds had built homes for their broods. Why couldn't she and John share a home and feed their family?

The diary with John's rosebud shared desk space with Vienna's texbooks. She had spent the past months in a daze, she realized. Had John believed her dead? Had he mourned her? Had he ever tried to find her?

With final exams coming up, she needed to master difficult subjects. She would make her family proud, no matter what. The twins' hard-earned money must be put to good use. She'd never be able to show her face to Elisha if she didn't make top grades. The boy looked up to her, his only sister.

The school bell rang, and Molly returned from her guitar lesson. Putting the instrument away, she addressed Vienna in her abrupt manner. "Let's talk about John."

Vienna's head snapped up. "What about John?"

"When you were jealous of me on the wagon train, why didn't you tell me to keep my hands off him?" Molly challenged. "I had no idea he was spoken for."

Vienna burst into tears. "If John wanted you, he could have you."

"I'm sorry I broached the subject, Vienna, but I want this matter cleared up between us."

"There's nothing to clear up, Molly. John assured me that I was needlessly jealous."

"I almost snatched John away from you." Molly appeared upset. "I made him pay attention to me, and you say there's nothing to clear up? Not only that, but I snatched Phil away from you too. Phil would marry you in a flash."

Vienna shook her head. "Phil and I aren't right."

"What about Zeke?" Molly asked.

"You know about Zeke?"

"Phil and Zeke are friends. Didn't you know?"

"Since when?"

"Since the day they saw you at the dry-goods store."

"Oh?" Vienna's head buzzed.

"Phil and Zeke acquired land in the South Bay. They're starting farms in the Santa Clara Valley." Molly's face grew animated. "Marry Zeke, Vienna. He desperately needs a wife. You'll love the Santa Clara Valley. Lots of sunshine and pleasant breezes. The scenery is pretty with oak trees and scalloped hills. Pa says anything will grow in that rich bottom loam. We could be neighbors, Vienna."

"I'm sorry, Molly. I'd love to be your neighbor, but I'm not ready to marry Zeke—or anybody else."

Molly grew intense. "Marry Zeke before it's too late, Vienna. Don't say I haven't warned you."

"What do you mean?"

"I mean before he's promised to somebody else."

"Like who?"

"Like Fran."

"The wheezing girl?"

"Marry Zeke right after graduation, Vienna. Tell him

now!" Molly turned and left the room.

Zeke and Fran? Vienna felt dazed. What did the two have in common? Zeke was protective, she remembered. Zeke loved to fuss over a girl. He'd make the ideal husband for Fran, the girl who had been bounced from room to room and wound up sleeping by herself over the delivery entrance.

Zeke never went for Priscilla, Vienna reflected. Zeke never paid attention to Molly, and she herself had resented being fussed over. Zeke was a godsend for Fran, the helpless girl. Fran would love and cherish Zeke and the home he offered. Where had the two met? Without a chaperone, Fran wasn't allowed out. During nights when the donkey brayed out front, was Zeke perhaps throwing messages up to Fran's window? Did she toss answers down to him? Vienna remembered rumors she had dismissed as idle gossip.

She recalled Zeke's motto: "Ain't no man gonna wait three years for a woman." Apparently, Zeke was acting on his belief.

During the night Vienna mulled over Molly's words. Molly would have yielded. She, Vienna, had withdrawn on the wagon train, feeling jealous and hurt. She had withdrawn again at the BIG Z, instead of asking John's mother about the identity of the lucky girl. Anger at herself exploded in Vienna's chest.

"If anybody has a right to John, it's me! I have first rights to his affections because he proposed to me first!" In a fit of helpless rage, she voiced her thoughts out loud.

Priscilla stirred in the bed across from her. "Did you say something?" she mumbled sleepily.

"If I had another chance I'd fight for my man, or at least clarify my position." Vienna was speaking more loudly than necessary.

Priscilla yawned and turned to the wall. Her even breathing and Molly's occasional snoring in the upper bed eventually lulled Vienna into a fitful sleep.

At the height of final exams Mrs. Graham dropped by for a surprise visit. Priscilla screeched with delight. "Come along, Vienna," she pleaded. "Give yourself a break. If you relax a little you'll accomplish more afterward."

Vienna hated to take time out during exams, but she finally yielded to Priscilla's urging. Maybe, just maybe, she'd see John and give him a piece of her mind.

The governess accompanied Priscilla and Vienna to the carriage where Mrs. Graham waited. "Where is Molly?" she asked.

"I didn't invite her," Priscilla said, climbing into the carriage.

"Why not?" her mother asked.

Priscilla whispered into her mother's ear, giving Phil on the high seat a withering glance.

Mrs. Graham snapped her umbrella shut. "Why, Phil!" she exclaimed. "Congratulations!"

Phil turned around, smiling broadly beneath his jet-black mustache, his violet eyes shining. "Is it all right, Ma—I mean Mother?"

"I am delighted, son. I feared you'd never show interest in girls. You are making your pa proud. A bride and a farm, that's what he wanted for you."

"What about Mr. Graham—I mean Daddy? Doesn't he want me to become a banker?"

Mrs. Graham laughed. "You, a banker? We've known all along you're not cut out for banking. Your daddy will help you all he can to start your farm."

Mrs. Graham left the carriage and strode to the porch of the school, lifting her skirts on the steps. She called for Molly at the entrance. "I will vouch for my future daughter-in-law," she told the governess.

Molly appeared, looking uncertain. "You called for me, Mrs. Graham?"

"My dear Molly, I certainly did!" Molly received Mrs. Graham's warm embrace and was ushered to the carriage.

Vienna caught Molly's happy look and felt a stab deep inside her heart. Mrs. Graham had been like a second mother to her. It could be she who was being welcomed into the family—if she had elected to marry Phil.

"Sit beside Phil, my dear girl," Mrs. Graham invited.

Molly climbed up with vigor and beamed at Phil. The two exchanged happy glances.

Priscilla pouted. "You'd think she was a queen."

"Giddyup!" Phil clucked to the horses with gusto. The carriage clattered over the gravel drive and entered the street.

The countryside had covered itself with yellow and blue wildflowers. Spring had truly arrived in all its glory. And there, in the middle of it all, was a golden chestnut horse, tied to a hitching post in front of a hotel.

"Stop, Phil! Stop!" Vienna shouted.

Before Phil could even set the brake, Vienna jumped from the carriage. Forgetting she was supposed to act like a lady, she ran toward the hotel.

"Wait for me!" Priscilla called, running after her.

Vienna whirled around. "Go back! Don't you *dare* come along! This time I'll do my own talking."

She crossed the street, then mounted the wooden sidewalk. The horse looked like Old Bess, the mare John had ridden in Indian country. The mare pricked up her ears, regarding Vienna with alert eyes.

Vienna peered past the swinging doors into the hotel lobby. Odors of whiskey and tobacco smoke assaulted her nose. In the dim light, she saw three men playing cards around a table. Dare she go inside? She pushed into the reek of smoke and stale air. The mustachioed man behind the bar raised his bushy eyebrows when he saw her. She didn't care. It was now or never!

"That horse outside—does it belong to Mr. Zumwalt? Is John Zumwalt staying here?"

The proprietor casually wiped a glass and held it up against the light. Then he pointed to the staircase.

"That's him, Missy."

Vienna gulped. John was coming downstairs, eyes riveted on her. He was even more handsome than she remembered. Heart hammering in her throat, she strode toward him. "John!"

He paused for one unbelieving second, then rushed toward her. "Vienna, is this really you, or am I seeing things?"

"It's me, and don't you come any closer!" Vienna cried.

"Vienna, my darling!"

"Don't you darling me!" she snapped. "I've waited for you going on five years. Why didn't you ever come for me?"

"I *have* looked for you, and I *did* find you, my darling," he said softly.

"Where? When? How? Explain!" Vienna demanded.

"After our wagons descended the Sierra Nevada, I waited for you at Sutter's Fort, but your wagon never came. Reason told me that you were snowed in somewhere in the mountains. I went up with search parties whenever there was word of somebody being snowed in. But it was never you."

"We didn't come over Donner Pass," Vienna said.

"I learned of another pass and traveled up to Marysville and Bidwell Bar after the terrible winter rains of 1852 and 1853. I asked for you everywhere. Nobody knew your name. Nobody had heard of a woman with six children passing through."

Vienna let him continue.

"Recalling that you had mentioned a sawmill at Berry Creek, I rode there during the summer of 1853. No sawmill existed." His eyes filled with tears. "I rejoined my brother and dear old mother in Sacramento. We burned our wagon and eventually settled east of San Francisco Bay. This is where I started my business."

"You never looked for me again." Vienna spoke with bitterness.

"To the contrary, my darling. I searched for you in

many places. In my heart, I could not accept that my vivacious girl might be dead. I prayed that, no matter what, your life was spared."

Vienna was beginning to feel faint. "But you never found me."

"I almost did at Bidwell Bar during the opening celebration of the new suspension bridge. People traveled from miles away to see the event. I so hoped to find you there."

"And then?"

"My search for you finally proved successful, my darling. I met your twin brothers, Elisha and Elijah, and I also saw your father."

"Did Elisha give you a message from me?"

John nodded. "Yes, he told me where you were."

"Then why didn't you ask for me at the academy?"

"I called at the academy many times. I was turned away in the severest manner."

"The governess never mentioned you!" Vienna exclaimed.

The gamblers noisily threw their cards on the table and raised their heads amid swirls of blue smoke. Vienna covered her mouth. She had completely forgotten about the people around her. And now Mrs. Graham was coming through the swinging doors.

"Just what are you doing in this dreadful place, John? I feel so ashamed being seen here."

"I rented a room, intending to stay close to the school through your graduation. I desperately feared I might miss you again."

"Why are you telling me all this?" Vienna challenged. "I spoke with your mother. She said you're engaged to be married."

He looked puzzled. "Did you tell her who you are?"

"N-no."

"Why not?"

"She, uh, didn't seem to like me."

"Nonsense! I've spoken about you in glowing terms."

"What about your engagement?" she pressed. "Who is the girl that came between us?"

John threw his head back and laughed heartily. "Why, you're jealous, my dear Vienna."

"Who is she?" Vienna hoped she wasn't going to faint. His eyes looked the bluest blue she'd ever seen, and she was melting inside. How long could she stand up to him?

"The girl to whom I am engaged is—and always has been—Vienna Brooks."

The floor seemed to give way beneath Vienna's feet. When she came to, she lay in her dormitory bed. A black-suited man stooped over her, pressing the end of a long, wooden cylinder to her chest and holding his ear to the other end, listening for her heartbeat.

"Nothing to be concerned about," he told the governess who stood beside him. "Nothing but a case of nerves." He fitted the listening device into a leather bag, then both left the room.

Priscilla entered, looking uncertain and concerned. "How are you, Vienna dear?"

"What happened to me, Priss?"

"You fainted. Meeting John was too much for you, you poor thing."

"How did I get here?"

"Mother became concerned when you didn't come out of that hotel. She went inside and found you in the arms of a young man. It was John. He made sure we brought you safely to the school."

"Did they let him in?"

"Not a chance!" Priscilla laughed. "It's against the rules."

Chapter Fifteen
Blessings

The event Vienna dreaded was at hand: meeting John's mother. She grasped John's strong, warm hand for reassurance as he guided her into a cozy kitchen.

"Will she like me, John?"

Mischief danced in his sky-blue eyes. "The girl who scared off buffalo has no courage?" he teased.

"Mother!" he called. "Please come down."

Vienna's hands had felt cold and clammy ever since the early-morning buggy ride in pea soup fog. She could hardly believe that it was only yesterday she, as class valedictorian, had given the farewell address at the academy's commencement exercises. And now she was with John.

Mrs. Zumwalt, tall and stately, entered the room. She did not seem pleased to see Vienna.

"Mother, this is the girl I want you to meet," John said.

"It seems that we have met already," Mrs. Zumwalt replied icily.

"You don't understand, Mother. This is *Vienna Brooks,* the girl I met on the wagon train. We're asking for your blessing."

Mrs. Zumwalt took a deep breath. "Leave us," she ordered John. Then, facing Vienna, she asked, "Where is your friend, the redhead, today?"

Vienna swallowed. "Priscilla went home to San Francisco. Her father is a banker there."

"Why do you keep company with that girl?"

"We were roommates, ma'am. She's really a very nice girl, only she acts silly at times. I've known her since we were neighbors in Michigan."

"You lived near a banker?"

"No, ma'am. Her father was a farmer. He died on the trail. Her widowed mother married a banker out here."

"My husband also died," Mrs. Zumwalt said slowly. "I am a widow. I have only John and his younger brother left. John has provided a secure place for us, the first home we've known since leaving the States. I don't want to lose John."

Vienna noticed the woman's resemblance to John, blue eyes under generous brows, an adorable widow's peak, the same square, determined chin. Suddenly she felt great tenderness for this woman who had given birth to her beloved.

"Oh, my dear Mrs. Zumwalt, I'll never take John away from you. I know you need him. But perhaps you also need a daughter to take care of you when you're sick."

"You would take care of me? I have sick headaches, you know."

"Oh, I know! John told me. He's ever so concerned about you. You need a dark and quiet place until the pain subsides. You need special care."

Vienna grasped the older woman's hand and rubbed it. "I shall sit by your side and warm your hands. I shall bring you herbal tea. I shall wait on customers and tell them to be very quiet, so as not to disturb you."

Mrs. Zumwalt's eyes swam with tears. "You would do all this for me?"

"This and more! I took good care of my father. He got the ague in the Michigan swamps, you see. He says I'm the best little nurse." Vienna detailed how her father's health had worsened. "Father worked on the farm. He built us cabins, the first in St. Joseph County, then another one at Bidwell Bar. He used to swing himself into the saddle, and he galloped away to California."

Vienna's voice broke. "Now he's an invalid. He walks on crutches. Sometimes he shakes with fever and we fear losing him. But that isn't all that concerns me," she added. "There are my brothers; I now have seven of them. With some education the oldest, Elisha, could be anything he wanted to be, but he cannot read. He could be a teacher! Instead, he's working at a sawmill." She couldn't hold back her stinging tears any longer.

John's mother took the girl into her soft arms. Cradling her like a baby, the older woman said, "You poor, poor child. Everything will be all right, you'll see."

Vienna felt comforted. Her own mother had cradled her like this in the Michigan shake cabin. For a delicious moment she felt that same bond and oneness with John's mother. She blinked away hot tears. "Then you'll give us your blessing?"

"My blessing and whatever else you need." Mrs. Zumwalt gently released the girl. "John!" she called.

"Yes, Mother?" John entered lightning-quick.

She pointed to the white-scrubbed plank floor. John knelt down and Vienna joined him.

"Promise before God that you will love and cherish this child," Mrs. Zumwalt told her son.

"I promise, Mother."

"In sickness and in health you will support her."

"Yes, Mother."

"And you, Vienna Brooks, promise to love and obey John and stand by him in sickness and in health."

Vienna bowed her head. "I do."

"You have my blessing. You may both get up."

John rose and gave his mother a huge hug. "We must leave you for now, Mother. We need another blessing, from Vienna's parents."

"Wait!" Mother Zumwalt hurried upstairs. She returned with a lacy bodice. "This is part of my wedding dress, children. It's all I managed to salvage coming across the Plains. Do you want it, Vienna?"

"Oh, yes! I'll wear it with pride."

Mother Zumwalt embraced her. "I hope you'll be as happy as I was on my wedding day."

Vienna added the bodice to gifts she'd received from friends and teachers. Her bag bulged with lacy odds and ends. If Mother was agreeable, she'd help her sew the wedding dress.

John's younger brother drove the couple to the riverboat bound for Sacramento and Marysville. Gray fog soon yielded to white clouds in a sea of blue sky. At Marysville they transferred to the stagecoach, which took them to Orovillle, Butte County's thriving new county seat. John rented a buggy, and Vienna directed him to the Brookses' place.

As they neared the cottage that overlooked the garden, John fell silent. Was he as worried as she was? Vienna wondered. Would her parents give them permission to marry? Would they give their blessing? At the cottage, John helped her out of the buggy.

A slim, tall woman appeared in the doorway. Mother! She was balancing a plump baby on her hip. The blond boy beside her let go of her skirt and ran toward Vienna, who swept him into her arms and hurried toward the cottage.

"I'm home, Mother!" she cried, hugging Mother and the baby all at once.

Embraces over, Mother's gaze focused on John.

Vienna set down little Jay and stepped beside her fiancé. "Mother, you remember John. We found each other at long last. We came to receive your blessing."

"Come in, both of you. Father is busy in the wood shop." Mother lit a candle in the darkening cottage, and they sat around the table. Mother looked troubled. "George, we have company!" she called.

Father entered on crutches. His clothes, hair, and beard

were covered with sawdust and wood chips. His sharp gray eyes brightened at the sight of Vienna. Then his brow furrowed on seeing John. "Who's he?" he asked bluntly.

Vienna gave her father a quick hug. "This is John, Pa, the young man I met on the wagon train. John and I need your blessing. We want to get married."

John sprang to his feet and extended his hand. "John Zumwalt, sir. We came to receive your blessing, sir."

Father ignored John's hand. "What are your circumstances, young man? Can you support a wife and family?" He sounded gruff.

John cleared his throat. "With all due respect, I have built up a dry-goods-store business in Oakland, a city on the eastern shore of San Francisco Bay. The house is small—two stories, with an upstairs room for my mother, and a room for my younger brother and myself. Downstairs are the salesroom, storeroom, a small office, and the kitchen. My business is doing well, sir, and there's plenty of space to add another room or two."

"How do we know you're worthy of our daughter?" Father demanded. "My wife raised the girl in a God-fearing manner, and she has turned out well. Why, my little Vienna is the finest girl any man can hope to get."

"Father, you're not giving away a princess!" Vienna protested.

"It's true, kitten. Any man would want you for his bride."

John tugged at his collar. "You may inquire of my neighbors and business associates, Mr. Brooks, sir. All will tell you that I conduct business in an honest fashion, and that I care properly for my younger brother and dear old mother."

"Vienna is too young," Father declared.

Icy fingers clutched Vienna. "That's what Mother told John five years ago," she blurted. "I am 18 years old and well prepared to marry John. He's a fine and upright man and the only one I'll ever marry."

Mother put the two little boys to bed. When she

returned, she faced Father, speaking carefully. "John waited for our Vienna five long years, dearest. He asked for her hand on the wagon train. I told him that we would consider his proposal a few years hence should he still be interested. It is only right that we find out if he is the outstanding man Vienna says he is."

Father eased himself onto the bench beside Vienna. "Bring something to drink," he told Mother. "Can't you see that we're thirsty?"

Mother dipped tin cups into the water bucket and brought them to the table. Father, Vienna, and John emptied them quickly and asked for refills. Father emptied his second cup in one big gulp.

"Where do you want to get married?" he asked Vienna.

"Wherever you decide, Pa."

He shook his head. "We have neither room nor money for a wedding, and we have no dowry."

"We can hold the wedding at my place," John offered. "As for a dowry, Vienna is all the treasure I need."

Father shook his head. "Your place is too far. Travel is an ordeal for me, and it costs too much money. I will not give my consent unless I can walk my only daughter to the altar."

Mother took a thoughtful sip from her cup. "We can have an outdoor wedding right here in the garden, dearest. It won't cost much. We can send for the itinerant preacher and invite a few friends."

"You can construct a bower and some benches, Pa. You're good at that," Vienna added.

Father stroked his beard. "How much time do I have?"

"Long enough for John to add a room to his house for the two of us." Vienna blushed.

Father brightened. "It's done then. The wedding will be here," he decided. "You have my blessing, and Mother's too."

On her wedding day Vienna rose at dawn. The first ducks flew overhead, signaling the end of summer. The

126

woodsy air smelled fresh and clean. On cleared ground, the Grahams and Steeles had erected huge tents containing bedsteads, rag rugs, and chairs. Smaller tents housed Priscilla, Molly, Fran, John, and his brother Joseph under the pines. Except for the twins, and Mother Zumwalt, who opted to mind the store rather than risking a migraine attack while traveling, everybody had come. Vienna missed Elisha. She had planned to read the letter in her diary to him in a quiet moment. The boy's presence would have made this day perfect.

Molly and Fran had created a big, beautiful wedding cake. Priscilla's waxen flowers rambled along Father's bower, rivaling Mother's late roses in beauty. Sturdy benches, smelling of freshly cut wood, faced the bower. Vienna smiled. Once Father had caught the spirit, he really applied himself.

The camp stirred. Voices swelled to a happy chatter as the wedding guests awoke. White smoke and breakfast smells soon wafted through the pines. Vienna wasn't hungry. She walked down to the river.

Fish snapped at low-flying insects and birds chattered in shrubbery along the riverbank. Vienna remembered another river where she had fallen in love with John.

"My darling!" John's voice sounded soft as a breeze behind her. "I followed you. I couldn't sleep."

"In a few hours we shall be man and wife," she said.

"My beautiful bride." He lifted her fingertips and held them to his smooth chin. "When we met, I hardly dared believe that someday you'd be my darling wife." He flashed his dazzling smile, and she again experienced the exquisite feeling his presence sent skipping to the ends of her body. She searched his face, finding the same dear features she had loved all along.

"Oh, my dearest." Vienna stroked the full hair at his temples. He was glorious. The lines that betrayed sadness and sorrow had vanished. Happiness was written all over him.

His clear blue eyes caressed her. "Have I told you that my prediction came true?"

"What prediction?"

"That one day in California you'd unfold like a rosebud and turn into a full-blown beauty." His eyes twinkled.

"I still have your rosebud," she confessed.

"You kept it?" Not waiting for an answer, he guided her to the garden, where he broke off a fresh rosebud. "For you."

She held the rosebud to her nose, inhaling the delicate perfume.

"Well?" he asked.

"It smells sweet."

"Sweet, like you." He gently placed her hand against his warm cheek. "I love you more than you can imagine, my darling."

Overwhelmed by happiness, she didn't answer.

"Let us get ready, darling. The preacher mustn't wait."

Vienna's wedding dress made a fluffy mound on the table. She and Mother had worked on it for weeks, sewing together the pieces of lace given her by family, friends, and teachers.

Vienna slipped into the precious gown. Mother fussed with the buttons, pulling and tugging at ruffles and folds. Priscilla curled and coaxed Vienna's hair, then fitted the veil on her light brown curls. Both stood back, admiring their work of art.

"You're the most beautiful bride I've ever seen!" Priscilla exclaimed.

Mother's eyes shone as she nodded in agreement.

"Leave me, please," Vienna requested. "I need a quiet moment."

Reflecting on her long search for John, she knelt down and thanked God for her happiness. True love had overcome formidable obstacles, she realized, and God had given His blessing. She fastened the fresh rosebud at her throat. Radiant, she stepped outside to meet John.